'James?' sh

'I'm causing tr█████████
before making t████████████
important,' he said. 'It's █████
question. What shall I wear to Megan's party?'

Delyth giggled. 'All women have a different answer to that. Megan has a wide variety of friends and some of them will be wearing suits. Others will be in jeans. You'll just have to decide.'

She heard him sniff. 'If you gave me that kind of briefing on the ward I'd give you a real telling-off. You're supposed to make my life easy. Should I bring a bottle?'

'Doubt if it'll be that kind of party,' she told him. 'But you could take a bunch of flowers if you like.'

'Or descend from a helicopter with a box of chocolates! You know, social life in Africa was much simpler.'

Gill Sanderson is a psychologist who finds time to write only by staying up late at night. Weekends are filled by her hobbies of gardening, running and mountain walking. Her ideas come from her work, from one son who is an oncologist, one son who is a nurse and her daughter who is a trainee midwife. She first wrote articles for learned journals and chapters for a textbook. Then she was encouraged to change to fiction by her husband, who is an established writer of war stories.

Recent titles by the same author:

UNDO THE PAST
A FAMILY FRIEND*
A FAMILY AGAIN*
A FAMILY TO SHARE*

* *Loving Sisters* trilogy

SEVENTH DAUGHTER

BY
GILL SANDERSON

For my sister Wenda—with love.

First published in Great Britain 1999
Harlequin Mills & Boon Limited,
Eton House, 18-24 Paradise Road, Richmond, Surrey TW9 1SR

© Gill Sanderson 1999

ISBN 0 263 81794 6

Set in Times Roman 10½ on 11½ pt.
03-9909-56684-D

Printed and bound in Spain
by Litografia Rosés S.A., Barcelona

CHAPTER ONE

T ONLY happened occasionally, which made it hurt more. And when it did Delyth was never wrong. She knew with n absolute certainty that the young man in the bed in front of her was dangerously ill. He might die before morning. And yet she could find little wrong with him.

It was midnight, and she had been bleeped to admit him o Gregory Ward—a surgical ward—from A and E an hour go. He claimed his name was Birdie Jones, one of many oung street-dwellers, and he'd been knocked down by a it-and-run driver and brought in by ambulance. Apart from hock, abrasions and general bruising, he had a closed fracure of the radius—a broken arm.

'Don't think there's much seriously wrong with him,' the A and E registrar had cheerfully told her. 'We've put a laster on his arm and patched him up. But keep him in for a couple of nights for observation. Feed him a bit, and then ie can go out on the streets again.'

This was a hospital in the centre of London and there was omething she had been told more than once. 'We provide nedical care only. We cannot concern ourselves with social problems—we are not funded to do it.' Delyth knew this vas a harsh but necessary doctrine.

Now young Birdie was in her care. She had clerked him carefully and followed the set procedures, keeping a close eye on blood pressure, pulse, abdominal signs. All was as expected. Although thin, he wasn't malnourished. But the knowledge had come with the strength of a physical blow. Birdie was in real danger. She checked all her findings igain—what had she missed? Apparently nothing.

Delyth sighed. She was the humblest of doctors, a mer[e?]
house officer. She had only qualified a few weeks ago. Th[e]
correct procedure in case of doubt was to refer upwards, i[n]
this case to James Owen, the specialist registrar. But sh[e]
knew James had been at work since six that morning, an[d]
he wasn't going to like being disturbed.

So far she hadn't met him. For the past fortnight he ha[d]
apparently been away at a conference. Earlier today she ha[d]
seen him in the distance, walking rapidly across the war[d,]
white coat flying behind him. Even from a distance he gav[e]
an impression of energy, of determination. If it was possibl[e]
to work out such a thing from just one glimpse, Delyt[h]
decided he didn't look a man who easily put up with fool[s.]
She sighed again.

She had been told that she could learn a lot from th[e]
senior nurses, that their opinion was always worth askin[g.]
So she asked Sue Ashton, the staff nurse in charge at nigh[t,]
what James was like. How would he react to being di[s]-
turbed?

Sue was fortyish, married with three children who alway[s]
phoned to wish her goodnight before they went to bed. Sh[e]
smiled amiably. 'Dr Owen? He's gorgeous, Delyth. Sort o[f]
tall and lean and dark. He's a good doctor but he frighten[s]
me—he's all intense. Are you going to get him out of bed[?]
I hope you've got a good reason.'

As Delyth thought of it, the conviction struck her agai[n,]
stronger than ever. Birdie was ill. Whatever James Owe[n]
thought, she was going to call him. 'If he's in bed he'll hav[e]
to get up,' she said. 'Can I use your phone?'

The phone was picked up practically at once. 'My hous[e]
officer, Dr Delyth Price,' a dry voice said. 'Dr Price, yo[u]
are talking to a very tired man. He is also stark naked, dri[p]-
ping wet from the shower and has a small whisky in hi[s]
hand. He's on his way to bed. I hope this is important.'

It was an attractive voice. It was deep, with just a touc[h] of humour to it which she suspected could easily become cutting. He didn't sound angry—yet.

The feeling flashed back. Birdie was ill, she knew she was right. But how to explain this to the SR?

'I've just admitted a young man from A and E. He's a road accident victim, just generally knocked about and with a fractured radius. He's in for observation.'

'What have you done for him?'

She detailed the necessary procedures, knowing that she had done everything properly.

'And there are no adverse signs? No cause for worry? Why have you called me?'

This was the difficult part. Drawing a deep breath, she said, 'I think I've missed something. I don't know what, but I have. So I called you.'

There was a pause. Then he said, 'You are a doctor now, you know. There are decisions that you have to—that you must make. You can't have your hand held for ever.'

She could hear the iron in his voice, but didn't think he was angry with her—yet. 'I'm making a decision. I'm calling you.'

Now his voice was neutral. 'I'm on my way. Expect me in about ten minutes.'

Gregory Ward was on the fourth floor and Delyth waited near the entrance, expecting to hear the lift sighing upwards. But instead there was the patter of fast feet on the stairs— he was running upwards. In the dim light of the hallway she could see his open white coat, and underneath it a white T-shirt, jeans, trainers without socks. He had come in casual clothes. He moved well, like an athlete. Then, too quickly, he was up to her, facing her.

He wasn't even out of breath. She felt his presence and it was a shock to her. Inside her that distant voice which was never wrong told her that this man would have an effect on her. She was not sure what—it could be a bad one. But

she knew it, just as certainly as she knew that Birdie was
ill. The voice was never wrong. Her life and this man's
would be somehow intertwined. The knowledge frightened
her a little.

He was tall, lean, his hair dark brown and cut short. Even
when perfectly still, as he now was, there was that impression of poised energy. His face was unsmiling but he wasn't
angry. She felt him assessing her, waiting to give judgement. And she knew she wanted this man's good opinion.
Not just because he was her senior. She wanted him to…like
her. Delyth blinked. She had never felt this way about a
man so soon after meeting him.

'I don't really need to sleep,' he said wryly. 'What have
you got for me?' Hearing him speak again, it was yet another thrill for her. She thought a voice was more affecting
than simple good looks in a man. James's voice was deep,
musical, with a tiny trace of a northern accent.

He held out his hand. 'Missed meeting you this morning,
Dr Price. I'm sorry. I'm James Owen. I hope we'll work
well together.'

'I'm sure we will,' she murmured. His handshake was
firm but not forceful; it was their first bodily contact. The
thrill of it ran through her.

Now he was closer she could see his eyes were dark grey.
She saw them flick across her, noting her trim body, the
black hair now tied tightly in a French plait.

'Don't tell me, you're Welsh,' he said.

'You get no points for that diagnosis, not when I have a
name like Delyth Price.' She had to fight back.

'True. But doctors should never trust what is apparently
obvious. You have a Welsh voice, and if there is a Celtic
facial type then you've got it.'

This could turn into an interesting conversation, she
thought. He might have thought the same, but instead he
said abruptly, 'Let's have a look at this young man.' He

yawned as he spoke, and when she remembered what he had already done that day she felt guilty. But, no, she was certain.

They strode down the ward corridor together, she conscious of how she had to step out to keep up with him. She went through Birdie's story and offered him her neatly written-out notes, telling him which tests she had conducted, what observations she had made. They reached Birdie's bedside.

'You seem to have followed every procedure absolutely correctly,' he said, 'and the results you have don't seem too worrying. Why did you call me out?'

'I've missed something,' she said flatly. 'I'm certain I have.'

He looked at her but said nothing for a moment. Then he shrugged and said, 'Well, let's take a look.'

His examination was as thorough as hers had been. And his results were exactly the same. There was nothing life-threateningly wrong with Birdie. 'Let's go to the doctors' room and have a coffee,' he said, after one last sharp look at the comatose form between them.

She poured him a coffee and he sipped, before saying, 'There was no need to call me out. Possibly there might be something wrong with your patient, but it isn't obvious from any signs.' He looked perplexed. 'Quite frankly, I'm surprised. I wouldn't have thought you were the kind of person to call for help unnecessarily. You seem both confident and competent.'

She thrilled to the compliment but there was nothing she could say. She still had that sense that something was wrong, but there was no way she was going to tell him now. She realised how easily he was letting her down: other registrars would have been angry. 'I'm sorry,' she mumbled.

'Don't be. You did what you thought best.' He yawned

again. 'Bedtime but, don't forget, you can call me any time. Goodnight.'

He was gone, at the same speed with which he had arrived. Again, he didn't take the lift. She went over to the window and watched him walking quickly across the outside quad. He turned to see her looking at him and raised an arm in farewell. She blushed as she waved back.

'How did he take being called out?' asked Sue as Delyth collapsed into a chair next to her.

'He took it very well. There was nothing there. I was wrong.'

'He didn't tell you off?'

'No. Perhaps he wanted to. Or perhaps he was too tired.'

'I've never seen him too tired to do what he really wanted,' said Sue. 'He *is* gorgeous, isn't he?'

Delyth was too fed up to lie. 'Yes,' she said simply. She didn't wish Birdie any harm but she wished Dr Owen *had* found something wrong with him. Then he might think better of her. Still…he wasn't angry with her apparently.

She could have gone back to bed. If there had been any serious change in any of the patients Sue would have rung her. Instead, she occupied herself with simple clerical tasks then tried to doze in the doctors' room. At regular intervals she checked Birdie's condition. And at four-fifteen it happened. There was a sudden dramatic drop in his blood pressure. She looked, then fetched Sue to confirm her findings.

'If you don't send for the doctor, I will,' said Sue. 'This is an emergency all right.' So Delyth phoned him again.

His voice was sleepy. 'Owen here.' She had an unexpected vision of him in bed, but banished it at once.

'Sorry, Dr Owen, Dr Price here. That patient you saw—his blood pressure has dropped like a brick. It was OK five minutes ago, but it's going down fast.'

The sleepiness had gone. 'Right. Start phoning. We want

a theatre, an anaesthetist, and we want them fast. Prep him as best you can and I'll be there in five minutes.'

After one last look at the now obviously ill Birdie, she went to do as James had asked. He arrived as she was putting the phone down. He was dressed just as before, but there were drops of water on his face and hair, and she realised he had dipped his head in a basin or under the shower.

Together they went to see Birdie, and once again he eased back the blankets and examined the bruises. Gently he palpated the abdomen. 'Concealed haemorrhage doesn't necessarily show itself at once. You can lose up to half your blood volume without any change in blood pressure. I'll bet this man has a ruptured spleen or something and he's been bleeding internally. Perhaps we should have had an ultrasound scan or a laparotomy but—I agree with you—there didn't seem any need to open the abdomen. You've got his blood cross-matched?'

'And ordered,' she said.

'Good. I've a feeling we're going to need it. Come on, let's go and scrub up.'

Birdie's spleen was indeed ruptured, and they had to take it out. She had seen and assisted in a splenectomy before, but had never seen it performed with such speed. He wasn't slapdash, but swift. And he gave her the chance to watch and to help with the more simple procedures. But finally it was finished, and Birdie was moved into the recovery room.

James stretched and yawned. 'A good job well done. I'm going to have a coffee before I get out of these greens. You need one too, I suspect.'

She peeled off her gloves and threw them into the bin. The excitement of the operation was now over, the adrenaline no longer pumping through her system. Suddenly a vast fatigue fell on her. 'I do need a coffee,' she admitted.

He poured two cups, passing her one. 'Now we have a problem,' he said. 'I'm supposed to be the expert, you the lowly house officer. But you spotted something that I didn't. You were absolutely certain there was something wrong, weren't you? Even when I said there wasn't.'

It was a difficult question, but she mumbled an honest answer. 'Yes,' she said.

'I want to know why and how you—' He broke off. With his forefinger he lifted her chin and looked at her. It was an intimate and exciting gesture, and she loved it. 'You're in no fit state to give thoughtful answers, are you? Have you arranged to sleep in tomorrow morning?'

She tried to conceal her feelings as she pointed to the window. 'The sun's shining—it *is* tomorrow morning. But, yes, Matt Dee, the other house officer will be in and I'll have a few hours in bed.' She was sorry when he took his finger away.

'Fine. I'm not going to ask now, but there are things I want to know. Have you been to the clubroom? Can we meet there for half an hour tonight if you're not doing anything else? Say about nine?'

It was a completely unexpected invitation. Also unexpected was her rush of pleasure at it. 'I'd like that.'

'Good. Now I'm off back to bed.'

Before she could go back to bed she had notes to write up. Then there was one last look at Birdie, and she was off across the sun-splashed quad to the residence. As she climbed wearily to her room she passed the kitchen shared by the five young doctors on her floor. A voice shouted, 'D'you want a cup of tea, night-owl?'

'Love one,' she called back, without bothering to stop.

Quickly she undressed, the habits of a lifetime making her put her discarded clothes away neatly. Then she pulled on her dressing-gown just as there was a knock on the door. 'Come in, Matt.'

Matt Dee was her fellow house officer on the consultant Michael Forrester's firm. The two had come to St Helen's Hospital together and had formed a friendship based on mutual need. Occasionally it occurred to Delyth that Matt would like their friendship to progress to something deeper, but for the moment she had enough to deal with. He was broad-shouldered and blond-haired—unlike her, he was a native Londoner.

'Busy night?' he asked her, handing her the mug of tea and sitting on her bed.

'Interesting. I've just finished assisting with an emergency splenectomy. I had to turn the SR out of bed twice.'

Matt whistled. 'James Owen? I did a ward round with him yesterday. He's like a dynamo. Makes me tired just to watch him.'

'Any good?' asked Delyth, too casually.

Matt nodded. 'Knows his stuff and still has time for a word with every patient. Just cuts right down to essentials. I hope I turn out to be as good as he is.'

'So do I. Come on, Matt, off you go. You've got work and I need my beauty sleep.'

'Cast out of your bedroom again,' he said amiably, pulling himself to his feet. 'Delyth, a few of us are going to the Old Town Walls tonight—there's Singleton's Jazz Band playing. Fancy coming along?'

The Old Town Walls was a pub not too far away—she'd been there with a group once or twice before. She would have liked to have gone again, but remembered with a flash of pleasure that she was already meeting someone that night. 'Love to, but I'm meeting someone at nine. I'll try and catch the last few minutes, though.'

'See you there, then.' Matt sauntered out.

Clutching her tea, Delyth sat at the head of her bed. Her back propped against the wall, she looked round her tiny room. She supposed she was lucky to have it, to live here.

St Helen's Hospital was in the centre—the very centre—of London. She could walk to Soho, Hyde Park, along the Embankment. It was very different from the tiny village she'd been brought up in north Wales.

She finished her tea, picked up a towel and walked along to get a shower. She would have preferred a bath, but knew that once in it she'd sleep. There was still tea in the pot when she returned, though the others had gone, and she helped herself to another mugful. Then she went back to her room to sleep.

But she didn't. This had happened before. There was a stage of fatigue so deep that she just couldn't sleep. The others had told her of it happening to them. So she sat up in bed and tried to write home. She hadn't had chance since sending the first scratched note when she had arrived. And she had so much to write about—everything was so different here. A mixed residence for a start. She picked up her pen. She would only need to write one letter, to her parents. She knew her mother would photocopy the letter and send copies to anyone likely to be interested. Bronwen Price was efficient. With seven daughters she had learned to be.

Delyth looked round the tiny room she had now lived in for a fortnight. Lived? She had done little else but sleep in it. It was clean, quiet; had bed, chair, desk, drawers, wardrobe, washbasin. Oh, and a window, but not a big one. It was painted a trouble-free white. She supposed it was all right. When she'd first moved in she'd allocated herself exactly three hours' home-making time. She'd bought a tray for the window-ledge, a set of pot plants and matching bright rugs for floor and bed. Fixed to the wall was her best buy, a four-foot square of plywood covered with cork tiles. On it were pinned pictures of her family, of the landscape round her village. Now the place felt like home.

'Dear all,' she wrote, 'Eight in the morning, been up all night and such a lot has happened. I'm so glad I came...'

It had been a definite decision. She'd spent most of her life in rural Wales, trained in a Welsh university, done her elective in a cottage hospital, working with Alun Roberts, the local GP, who had helped her so much in her ambition. But when she'd finally qualified she'd decided she needed something different. Probably she'd spend the rest of her life practising in Wales—why not see something of the rest of the world? So she had come to this central, metropolitan hospital.

So far she had been made very welcome. Her consultant, the head of her firm, the man technically in charge of her further training, was Michael Forrester. She'd only met him twice. He seemed caring, but he had an international reputation and spent much of his time on committees and travelling abroad. Mostly, she would learn from the two specialist registrars, James Owen and Peter Kenny. The other house officer she knew. He was, of course, Matt Dee.

Matt came from Essex and had trained locally. He knew London well, was streetwise in a way she was not. She'd happily accepted his offer to show her round in the odd few hours they could get away.

All this she wrote, in her usual chatty way. The hard work, the long hours, the difficulty in understanding some people—and those who pretended not to understand her Welsh accent. 'This morning I got the SR out of bed—twice,' she wrote. 'He didn't like it much, but in the end I was right. He seems...'

She laid down her pen. How did James Owen seem to her? Perhaps she was too tired to examine her own feelings. She merely wrote, 'His name may be Owen but I don't think he's Welsh.' Then she went to sleep. Her last thought was that she was to meet him later. She was surprised at how happy it made her feel.

Because she had worked all night she was allowed a few hours' sleep, but she was back on the ward in the late afternoon and early evening. She was chatting to one of her patients who was about to be discharged, going through the seemingly interminable procedures that had to be followed and which were the special duties of the house officer.

She was getting a doctor's ear. There was the usual background noise to the ward—the rattle of feet, the hum of conversation, the tinkle of spoon on glass. And in the middle of it she heard a soft thump. A thump that shouldn't have been there.

Excusing herself, she darted into the next small room. On the floor by the bed lay an untidy pile of bedclothes, with a wizened head peering out of the top. Eighty-seven-year-old Mrs Ransome had fallen out of bed.

Calling for a nurse, Delyth knelt by the frail old lady. 'What am I doing down here?' Mrs Ransome asked, with some surprise. 'I was having a lovely dream.'

'Don't worry, Mrs Ransome,' Delyth said gently. 'Let's just make sure you haven't hurt yourself. You can get back to bed in a minute.'

With the shocked nurse's help she inspected Mrs Ransome for bruising or bleeding. Then she looked for fractures, looking especially at the wrist, hip and scaphoid bone—the one on the thumb side of the hand. Old people broke bones very easily, and the scaphoid bone was the one that fractured when people tried to stop a fall. But this time there were no breaks.

Gently, she and the nurse lifted Mrs Ransome back into bed then Delyth checked the old lady's temperature, blood pressure, pulse and respiratory rate. All were satisfactory. There was no need to assess the consciousness level on the Glasgow coma scale. Mrs Ransome never stopped chattering. She had apparently suffered no ill effects at all.

Delyth asked if side panels could be fitted to the bed, and wrote an account of the accident in Mrs Ransome's notes. She was given an accident form, which she completed and signed. Then she looked at her watch. Three quarters of an hour had passed. It was a busy life.

On the way back to her room she called at the canteen to buy a couple of sandwiches. She could eat them as she changed. She made herself the usual mug of tea and sat on her bed to consider. She was meeting Dr Owen in the Clubroom. It wasn't really what you would call a date, just meeting a senior colleague who wanted to get to know who he would be working with. After all, the consultant had taken her for coffee in the senior lounge. But she wanted to look—nice. There wasn't time to brush out her hair, but she tidied it. Then she put on black velvet trousers and a white silk shirt. A thin grey jacket in case it got cold later. As she set off she felt a throb of anticipation. Dr Owen was an attractive man.

She crossed the great quad, looking up at the red Victorian buildings on each side, then out of the main gate and into the busy London street. It still seemed strange to her, the hospital so close to the pulsing city centre. Down the road, past the vegetable stall that sold strange things she'd never tasted but had promised herself she soon would.

Affecting the casualness of a *habitué*—though she'd never been there on her own before—she entered the Saracen's Head. Bypassing the main bar, she walked down a dark corridor and pushed a door at the end under a sign saying No SMOKING. This was the Clubroom—the unofficial meeting place of the medical staff of St Helen's Hospital. Technically it was a public room, but it was used almost exclusively by doctors and nurses. It was a comfortable room, dimly lit, with no piped music or arcade games. The paper and upholstery were dark red, the woodwork ornately carved. The landlord had a soft spot for doctors. St Helen's had successfully treated his wife for cancer.

Though Delyth was new to the hospital, there were a few people she recognised. And there in a corner was James

Owen, standing to meet her. She didn't know what to make of the thrill she felt when she saw him, the dryness of her mouth and the shiver up her back. Probably nervous at meeting a senior man, she decided.

'Delyth, it's good to see you. It is Delyth, isn't it? And now we're off the ward you must call me James.' That gorgeous voice. Listening to it, it felt like being stroked by warm silk.

'You said the Clubhouse at nine,' she reminded him, then, hearing herself, added, 'Sorry, didn't mean to sound sharp.' What was wrong with her?

'No matter. You're here now. Sit in the corner there. What will you have to drink?'

'I'd like a white wine spritzer please, with chilled soda.' It was a drink to which Matt had introduced her, refreshing and only slightly alcoholic. As he went to order at the little window that opened into the main bar she glanced around again at the other people there. She had to admit it, there was an expression of curiosity on the face of a lady radiographer and frank envy from a gaggle of nurses.

She looked at James as he chatted to the landlord. He was still in jeans and a T-shirt. He looked like an athlete, she noted. There were no signs of a paunch. Too many male hospital doctors led disorganised lives, eating the wrong food at the wrong time, drinking too much alcohol and getting no exercise. By the time they reached thirty this life was having an effect. But not on James Owen. He looked well.

He came back with her spritzer and a beer for himself. 'One thing in the African bush I missed was good beer,' he said. 'There were imported wine and spirits, but only native beer. And it was horrible.'

She was interested. 'I didn't know you'd been to Africa.'

'Spent two years there, working in a rural hospital. No end of work, too. You have to move fast, but you learn a lot. I learned a lot of surgery there—but it's not a way to learn that I'd recommend to anybody.'

'Why not?' she asked curiously.

'No one to ask advice from, no one to consult. Professionally, you're alone. People think you have the answer and you know you don't.'

'So you weren't tempted to stay?'

The answer was long and drawn out. 'No-o.'

'Again, why not?'

He smiled at her. 'Look round a bit,' he said, indicating the rest of the room. 'This is the Clubroom. People come here to get away from the hospital—and they bring it with them. They're all talking about medicine.'

She let her ears take in the hum of conversations round her. He was right. 'We just need more beds…'

'Particularly tricky incision…'

'Not drug induced…'

'You're right,' she said. 'Aren't we a boring lot?'

There was a burst of giggling from the nurses in the corner, and a voice said, 'But the hem was far too low.'

'There you are,' Delyth said with some satisfaction. 'They're talking about dresses. Girl talk. It takes a woman to get away from work.'

He sniffed. 'I'm not convinced. I know that girl. She's a scrub nurse—she'll probably be talking about theatre gowns not ball gowns.'

They both smiled. She liked being with him, felt at ease with him. This surprised her. Usually she was a shy woman, rather in awe of her superiors. And James was an awesome man. So why did she feel so comfortable with him? 'You were going to tell me why you left Africa,' she reminded him. She wanted to know all about him—his history, what he liked, why he liked it.

He pursed his lips. 'Well, there was my career, of course. I want to make consultant in time, and, rather sadly, time in Africa doesn't seem to count for much. But, more important, I just got angry. I know I shouldn't have, I know it wasn't fair, I know a good doctor just accepts people as they are. But...'

He *was* angry, Delyth could tell. There was something about the set of his shoulders, the bleakness of his face. He was one of those frightening people whose voice got lower when they were angry—she was glad he wasn't mad at her. 'Go on,' she said.

She could see the conscious effort he made to relax. 'I didn't like the system there,' he said flatly. 'No, it's more than that. I just couldn't live with it. It's a fault in me. I should be able to distance myself from it, but I felt sympathy for the people involved.' He shook his head, as if to banish his bitter thoughts.

'Anyway, the last straw was when we had a lad brought in on an ox-cart. Name, Joseph. Problem, "pain in belly". It was a hell of a pain, too. I examined him. It wasn't a hard diagnosis—the lad had a hiatus hernia. I operated at once and sent him back to the ward, thinking I'd done a good job. Compared to ours, the wards were primitive—the rain used to rattle like fury on the tin roofs. But the staff were willing and competent. We were training them. Joseph was fine the next day. Told me he'd like to be a nurse or a doctor if it could be possible, and I encouraged him.

'Three days later I had to go to a village nearby to take a clinic. When I came back Joseph was gone. His mother had brought him in but his father had taken him out. There was nothing the staff could do. The father said they had no business interfering with a family matter.'

James paused and drank deeply from his glass. 'Did you ever see him again?' Delyth asked gently.

'I certainly did. A week later he was brought back again, weak, emaciated, his temperature sky high. I looked at the incision I'd made. Somebody had pulled off the dressing and smeared it with all sorts of muck. The infection had gone too far. In spite of massive antibiotics, he died two days later. It turned out that some local healer type had said that the problem was devils, and that he would scare them out of the belly. He took off my dressing, smeared on his own, and Joseph died.'

'Even in England people believe in some odd things,' she pointed out.

'Don't I know it. People read their horoscopes and believe in them. Medicine's affected too. There's an entire army of con artists, offering cures for what can't be cured. Fake faith healers. Loonies who wave crystals over you and divine your illness. People with the *power*!'

Delyth was beginning to feel slightly apprehensive. His obviously sincere anger worried her. She didn't entirely agree with everything he'd said, and she suspected she was shortly going to have to tell him so.

He turned to smile at her, his sombre expression gone. 'I'm sorry to get all agitated,' he said. 'It doesn't happen very often. Now, what I'm really interested in is how you saw something that I missed this morning. You were absolutely certain that young Birdie was ill, weren't you?'

'I…thought so,' she said weakly.

'But you did every possible test, and so did I. There was no indication at all. We all know that ruptured spleens often don't present straight away—that's part of the trouble. But you knew. How?'

The trouble was, she knew his interest was absolutely sincere. He *did* want to know, if necessary to learn from her. As he looked at her he moved nearer. She could feel the warmth of his body, his muscular forearm grazing hers. She liked him being so close, but she knew that what she was about to say would anger him. He hated what he called superstition.

'I just knew,' she offered. 'Call it woman's intuition.'

He shook his head decisively. 'Not good enough, Delyth. You weren't being intuitive—whatever that might be. You were absolutely certain. I want to know why.'

He frowned when she hesitated. 'I'm hoping to learn from you, Delyth. I like to think that I'm willing to learn from anyone. A doctor who thinks he knows everything is a positive danger.'

She had to try. 'I will tell you,' she said, 'but, please, don't tell anyone else. And don't laugh at me, and don't get angry at me.'

'Don't laugh at you and don't get angry at you? This is getting more and more intriguing.'

She sighed, thinking of what he had said about superstition. 'You'll think this is a Welsh old wives' tale, and I suppose it is. It doesn't happen very often. Sometimes I just…know that someone is seriously ill. I can feel it and I'm absolutely certain. And I've never been wrong. It's not the medical evidence—it's something from deep inside me.'

She paused, then looked at him accusingly. 'You're trying not to laugh. Or you think I'm a silly little girl.' She searched his blank face.

'A part of me thinks that,' he admitted. 'Quite a big part. But there was some proof. You diagnosed Birdie so I have to take you seriously. Tell me about another occasion it happened.'

She thought. 'Sometimes—often, in fact—it's obvious. The doctor in charge already knows. It's just that I know before I've read the notes or examined the patient. Once when I was a student, I was sent to a local hospital to observe. I was in A and E and it was Saturday—we were very busy. A girl was brought in, triaged and put in a cubicle. The nurse who saw her thought her case was serious but not life-threatening. I knew it was life-threatening. I tried to tell the doctor, but he told me not to be so silly. He was madly busy, had serious cases to see to. And he had. The girl died. She had a brain haemorrhage. There was no way of telling, but I knew.'

The horror of that night was still with her. It could be heard in her voice. He put his hand reassuringly over hers. 'Remember, Delyth, we're not gods. We do the best we can, but some we lose.'

He may as well have the full story, she thought. 'Now I'm going to annoy you,' she said. 'You know the seventh son of a seventh son is supposed to have magic powers?'

He nodded. 'Yes. It's a superstition I've heard.'

'Well, I'm a seventh daughter. And my mother was a seventh daughter too. Now you can laugh.'

Shaking his head, he said, 'I'm not going to laugh. I'm impressed. But I'm not going to believe you either. There was a famous case of a horse who could count. Show it two cards, one with the figure five and one with three on, and it would stamp its hoof eight times on the floor. Its owner—and other people—believed implicitly that it had read the cards. But what really happened was that the horse was watching its owner, and it saw him tense after the eighth stamp. It reacted to that subtle signal, and the owner never realised what was happening.'

'I'm not a horse,' she said.

'There are doctors who can tell what's wrong with a patient just with one look. It's not instinct, just lots of little clues they've picked up without realising. You've got that ability, but you've got it early. In time you'll be a brilliant diagnostician.'

Well, he hadn't laughed at her. His theory was a good one, but she still felt he was wrong. No matter, now they could carry on as… How were they going to carry on? she wondered.

He finished his beer. 'D'you want another drink? I've taken up your time. You might have other plans for tonight.'

She'd really like to sit here and talk to him. But they'd

only just met—she wouldn't be too forward. Still, she was certain she didn't want to part from him.

'I'd better not have another drink here. I've been invited to go to the Old City Walls with a group of young doctors. There's a jazz group there and I'd like to hear them.' She paused a moment, hoping. 'You could come if you liked.'

'If I liked?' He was teasing her.

'I'll rephrase that. I'd be glad of your company tonight and I'm sure everyone else would. Please, come.'

'I'd love to,' he said. 'Let's go.'

She was glad to sit down when they got to the pub. She thought of herself as a fit country girl, but James walked like one possessed. He had long legs, was a fast mover. When she mentioned it he slowed down—to just above a normal fast walk. 'Sorry,' he apologised. 'When I get time I do some running.'

Like all jazz pubs it was crowded, noisy and cheerful. She was squashed into a corner with Matt and others she vaguely knew. James got on well with everyone there, but she noticed a certain amount of deference to him. He bought a round of drinks, and she was interested at one stage to hear him telling Matt about the drum beating he used to hear in Africa.

When the band had played its last number, Matt and his friends decided to stay on. But Delyth told them she was tired and was going home. James offered to walk her back.

'This is so different from the silence at home,' she said as they paced through the London streets, still vibrant with night life. 'At this time most of my village is in bed.'

'Do you like London? Not too much of a culture shock?'

'Medicine here is a bit different,' she said cautiously. 'I sometimes think I ought to be a social worker as well as a doctor. And sometimes I think I should be a linguist too.'

'But what about the city itself?'

'I love it. It's so big and there's so much to do. It's so alive. I know I'll never see all I want to.'

They walked on in silence for a few moments. She noticed he'd moderated his pace and felt vaguely pleased. 'I've been in London since I was eighteen,' he said, 'apart from the two years I spent in Africa. Would you like me to show you something of the city—say on Saturday morning? I've looked at the roster. I know you've got a couple of days off.'

She was rather intrigued that he'd bothered to look up her off days. 'I've already arranged to go out with Megan, my sister on Saturday morning,' she said, 'but I'd love it if you'd come with us.'

He seemed rather taken aback by this. Only after a moment did she realise that he'd wanted her to himself. Wouldn't I be in the way?' he asked.

'Not at all. Megan would love to see you. The thing is...where were you thinking of taking me?'

He shrugged. 'London is full of places. I thought Covent Garden, maybe, or a walk in a park if it was fine, perhaps down the Mall.'

She would have liked all those things, but Megan had work to do. 'I've arranged with Megan to meet in the British Museum.'

'The British Museum!'

'Yes, well, Megan likes looking at the stone carvings there—and so do I. But don't come if you don't—'

'Stone carvings? Just a minute—is your sister Megan Price the sculptor?'

Delyth was rather pleased he had heard of her. 'Yes, as a matter of fact, she is.'

'Good Lord. I had no idea. I'd really like to meet her.'

They were now in the quad of the hospital. He walked her over to the residence, and she stopped outside. Formally, she said, 'I've enjoyed the evening and your company James. I won't invite you in because I'm tired.'

'I've enjoyed the evening, too, Delyth. I don't think I'v ever had a house officer like you. Shall we meet here at te on Saturday morning?'

He bent to kiss her briefly, like a friend. 'Goodnigh Delyth.'

He watched her as she walked into the residence lobb then turned to go. She started up the stairs then peered bac round the corner. He was walking away, fast again. Jame was driven.

She undressed and prepared for bed. Then she though about the kiss. It had been friendly, no more than that. Sh thought she wanted more. James had affected her more tha any other man she'd ever met. But she didn't know wha she meant to him.

CHAPTER TWO

DELYTH enjoyed it, but life as a house officer was hard. The idea was that she learned on the job. Instead of listening, watching and questioning as she had as a student, now she had to make decisions. At times she was unsure.

She started next morning by doing the bloods, taking specimens and sending them for analysis. Often it was easy, sometimes it was not. There were more than a few drug addicts on Gregory Ward, most of them having injected themselves so often that their veins had just shut down. If necessary she could call on the services of a professional phlebotomist, a middle-aged woman who did nothing but tour the wards, taking blood. But Delyth wanted to be able to do the job herself so she persevered.

There was the usual mass of paperwork. Then there was time for some real medicine. She had to clerk the day's intake of patients. She was soon reminded that there was nothing minor about any procedure in hospital.

Wendy Webster, a rather stout woman aged about fifty, had come in for the most minor of operations. She was to have a phlebectomy, her varicose veins taken out. As with all non-life-threatening operations there had been a waiting list, but Wendy's appointment had now come.

'I've had to wait an awful long time, Doctor,' Wendy complained mildly, 'and I've been feeling very tired lately. D'you think I'll feel better afterwards?'

'You should move a lot more comfortably,' Delyth said. 'We'll just have to see.' She had been warned against promising patients that all their problems would be solved after their operations.

After writing down the basic information Wendy offered Delyth examined her patient's legs. The veins were prominent, and Delyth performed a Trendelenberg test, raising each leg to drain it and then applying tourniquets so that when Wendy stood she could remove them and note the level at which the vein filled with blood. Then she identified the perforators in the veins by placing the Doppler probe over the calf and compressing the flesh until she could hear the hiss of venous blood. Her conclusions were carefully noted.

'We'll finish with a general look at you,' Delyth said. 'It would be a pity to miss anything.' She carried on with her overview examination, checking and noting Wendy's respiratory, neurological and cardiovascular systems. For her age and weight, Wendy was in reasonable shape. There seemed to be no reason she shouldn't have a general anaesthetic.

'Now, if you'll just slip down your nightie, I'll check your breasts,' Delyth said finally. She glanced at the notes. 'I see you've never had a mammogram or a smear test.'

'I've had enough trouble with my legs,' Wendy said firmly. 'I don't want to spend all my time at the doctor's. My GP suggested it, but I told him I didn't want to bother.'

This was not an uncommon reaction, Delyth knew. Too many patients felt that if they had one illness they were mysteriously prevented from contracting another. 'It's always a good idea to have a test,' she said gently. 'It gives you peace of mind. Do you ever check your breasts yourself for lumps?'

Wendy didn't. She indicated that she felt it wasn't quite ladylike.

'Never felt any pain there? No discharge, no alteration in shape or size?'

'Nothing, Doctor. Apart from my legs, I'm fine.'

Carefully, Delyth palpated each breast in turn. And there

the left breast, was a lump—with that unmistakable gritty
el that suggested cancer. She managed not to let the dis-
ay she felt show on her face.

There were other questions and tests to follow. She felt
e lymph nodes in Wendy's armpits, asked about breath-
ssness, loss of weight, palpated the abdomen.

'There'll be someone else to see you in a while Wendy,'
e said finally. 'You can pull up your nightie. That's all
r the minute.'

'I'll be glad when these veins are done,' Wendy said.
hen I can start enjoying life again.'

'That's the spirit,' Delyth agreed.

Earlier on, Peter Kenny, the other specialist registrar, had
me on the ward. He had nodded to Delyth in his usual
ther abrupt way and asked her for the case notes on a
tient. Now she found him in the doctors' room, drinking
ffee and writing up his examination.

'I've just clerked Wendy Webster,' Delyth said. 'She's
 your list for a phlebectomy tomorrow.'

'Quite so. Do you want to assist?'

'There's a lump in her breast. I'm pretty sure it's can-
rous.'

Peter put down his pen. 'I see. What tests have you
ne?'

She shook her head. 'Just the usual examination. And I
rtainly haven't told her what I suspect. Wendy thinks
e's here for a simple operation on her legs. She's bound
 wonder what's wrong if we start messing round with the
her end of her.'

'That's true. Well, I'd better come and have a look and
 'll think about a mammogram and a fine needle aspiration
opsy. Then we'll decide if we want an oncologist to see
r.'

Delyth nodded. Once they had an X-ray of the lump and
d taken a tiny sliver of it for laboratory examination,

they'd know what they had to do. '"In any examinati
always check the breasts",' she quoted. 'I certainly kn
why now.'

'Finding something you don't expect is always a sho
I'm afraid you'll get used to it, though.'

Peter had the reputation of being competent but rat
distant. Delyth was finding him sympathetic.

She didn't see much more of James. He waved to her on
when he was visiting someone in the ward, but she was bu
herself and had no good excuse to go and speak to him. .
ever, he was moving fast. She remembered her earlier ide
about him—he was driven.

'What was James doing on the ward?' she asked St
Nurse Ashton, well aware that her apparent casualne
wasn't fooling the shrewd sister at all.

'Just wanted to check on Birdie Jones's condition,' S
said comfortably. 'I'm surprised he didn't come over to a
you about him.'

'I was trying to get in touch with Wendy's husband. H
left a daytime contact number, but his firm couldn't fi
him. They seemed to think it was my fault.'

'It's always the doctor's fault. Anyway, James had to ru
off to a clinic at one of the other hospitals. Good-looki
man, but he doesn't seem ready to settle down yet, does h
I've seen him with one or two ladies, but nothing ever ca
of it.'

Delyth recognised that this was a delicate and well-me
warning. 'Perhaps he just hasn't yet found the right woma
she suggested.

'Perhaps.' Sue wrinkled her forehead and rubbed her ey
with her palms. 'There was something I heard about h
before he went to Africa... I can't remember—not a scand
a tragedy. I was away at the time so it didn't concern m

'You can't remember?' asked Delyth, trying to conceal er interest.

'It'll come back to me. Mind you, there's always gossip hospitals, and most of it is untrue.'

'Isn't it just?' said the disappointed Delyth. She wanted know as much about James as possible.

aturday morning came with warm, early September eather. Delyth dressed in jeans, a dark shirt and flat shoes. ny museum trip with her sister was likely to involve lots f walking.

It didn't surprise her that James wasn't waiting for her, anding in the sun or sitting on a bench. Instead he was acing along the side of the quad, looking up at the fine red rickwork. Like her, he was dressed casually, in jeans, polo irt and a light jacket. For a moment she had time to study is face before he noticed her. There was a bleakness there, e thought, almost a sadness. She wondered why as she alked to his side. 'I'm not late. I'm exactly on time.'

His face changed when he looked at her, obviously leased to see her. 'True. And I suspect you're never un- unctual.'

He took her arm and turned her towards the gate. 'Let's . There are lots of ways of getting about central London— xis, the Tube, buses, even bikes—but the one most people em to forget is walking.'

'I like walking,' she told him, 'but not always at your te.'

'Sorry. Sometimes I forget.' They strode off together. 'It's nly fifteen minutes to the British Museum.'

There weren't quite as many tourists outside the museum there had been in high summer, but still the broad steps ere covered with them, chattering in a dozen languages d industriously photographing each other. Delyth and mes threaded their way upwards.

Delyth had arranged to meet her sister in the shop ju
inside the entrance; as ever, Megan had bought a doze
postcards. The two girls were recognisably sisters, eve
though Megan was ten years older than Delyth. Her dar
hair was cut fashionably short and she was dressed stri
ingly as always, all in black with a barbaric silver necklac
There was a large notebook and pencils stuffed into th
pocket on her thigh. Megan never moved far without he
sketchbook.

After kissing her sister, Delyth introduced James. The tw
looked at each other warily. 'You're older than Delyth
Megan said abruptly.

He smiled. 'I like big sisters who look after little sisters
he said. 'I'm only about eight years older.'

Megan relaxed. 'I'm sorry, I can't get over treating he
as an innocent child in the evil city. I'm pleased to me
you.' She waved her hand in one of her imperious gesture
'Is there anything you particularly want to see here?'

'Everything. It's terrible to admit, but I've never bee
here before. I visit all the art galleries and the V and
regularly, but never here.'

'You'll never take it all in in one visit. You need to com
regularly. The Assyrian statues—'

'Why did *you* particularly want to come?' Delyth brok
in. 'You said there was something you needed to look at.

'I've been commissioned to do a bronze for the entranc
hall of a company that trades a lot with Egypt and th
Middle East. I've come looking for inspiration.'

'We'll follow you,' James said. 'And when you want
stand and think a while then we'll wander on.'

'Yes,' said Megan thoughtfully, 'that's a good idea.'

After strolling through galleries devoted to twentiet
century art, they eventually came to one that featured earl
art from Saudi Arabia. Here they stopped. Delyth could te

hat Megan was excited by what she saw. Her eyes were
ixed on a bronze ibex, her replies to their questions shorter.

James winked at Delyth. 'Why don't we wander on round
and meet you later?' he asked Megan. 'You obviously want
to study this for some time.'

'Mmm? Sorry, oh, yes,' mumbled Megan. 'In the café in
about an hour, then.' As they walked away she had pulled
out her sketchpad and was already slashing the first bold
strokes across it.

Delyth sighed with exasperation and fondness. 'She's always like this. In fact, all my sisters are like it. They're all
artists of some sort and they're all single-minded. She
doesn't mean to be rude.'

'I didn't think she was being rude. I like people who
now what they want.' After a while he asked, 'So, why
aren't you an artist too?'

She shook her head decisively. 'Never any chance of it.
I like a lot of the things my sisters like, but I knew medicine
was for me from when I was very young. I never even
thought about anything else.'

'Interesting,' he murmured. 'I didn't make my mind up
ill later.'

She was enjoying herself. He was a good companion to
walk round a museum with, always ready to stop and talk
about what they were viewing. They moved to the stairs and
paused to look at a magnificent collection of bronze plaques.
He frowned as he read the account of what they were seeing.

'I remember these,' he said. 'They were originally cast
about a hundred miles from where I worked.'

She was surprised. The thought didn't seem to please him.

'Delyth, how could the people who created these not progress further?'

'You're thinking about that boy who died,' she said. 'You
know doctors can never ask why people apparently get

themselves into trouble. We help when we can. Everyone'
flawed—we have to expect that and include ourselves.'

'I know, Delyth, I know! It just…angers me at times
That boy's death was an unnecessary waste of a life. An
all through superstition.'

'People need to believe,' she said, 'and it's not up to u
to tell them what to believe. Come on, let's go and lool
through here.'

Five minutes later he had apparently forgotten the foll
of superstition and was fascinated by the intricate pattern or
the side of a primitive bowl. She liked him for his enthu
siasm. Too many of the older doctors she had met cultivate
a world-weary attitude, probably as a way of dealing wit
the problems they saw. Not James. As she had told hersel
before—he was driven.

Her legs were weary before his were, and she had t
remind him that they were to meet Megan in the café. Sh
waved to them as they entered. James fetched a tray o
sandwiches and tea and the three of them sat in a corner.

Megan's preoccupation had disappeared. Waving a sand
wich, she told them happily that she had made a doze
rough sketches and that a basic idea was emerging. 'It
based on that carving of a boat I saw,' she told them. ')
was an incense burner. But it'll be quite different. Now
know where I'm going I can relax.'

She turned to look at James more closely. With a sinkin
feeling Delyth realised that Megan had decided that it wa
time to turn all her attention on the slightly older man he
little sister had brought along. 'Did you enjoy your visi
James?' she asked.

'Very much so. It's now on the list of places I'll visi
regularly.'

'That's good,' said Megan. 'Which places in Londo
don't you visit regularly?'

He wasn't upset by this odd question. 'Parliament,' h

answered promptly, 'especially the House of Commons. It's full of people apparently not getting anything done.'

'You believe you could do better?' Megan pressed him.

'Sometimes I feel I could cut a lot of unnecessary talk and get on with things. It's a doctor's fault. We all think that we can do better than everyone else.'

Delyth decided to try to save him from a further inquisition. 'That's because all the young nurses and doctors look up to you and think you're marvellous,' she said.

He sighed mournfully. 'If only that were true. A man can dream.' He looked at his watch. 'Ladies, I have to go. There's work waiting for me and I know you two have a lot to talk about.' He stood and offered his hand. 'Megan, I've really enjoyed meeting you. I hope to see you again some time.'

Megan smiled the sweet smile which, Delyth knew, hid a quickly calculating mind. 'It could be sooner than you think,' she said. 'I'm having a little party tonight. Delyth's coming. Would you like to come too? Nothing formal, just a couple of dozen friends.'

Delyth felt his questioning look on her. 'Do come,' she said. 'We could share a taxi. I'm *not* going to walk in my best outfit.'

'Then I'd love to come.'

'Arrive about nine,' Megan said, obviously pleased. 'Delyth knows the address—it's on top of Crouch Hill.'

'Looking forward to it.' He rested his hand on Delyth's shoulder a moment and then he was gone, striding rapidly between the tables. The two sisters watched him in silence.

Delyth poured herself some more tea. 'Are you going to do the big sister act?' she asked with a grin. 'Either tell me off or ask me if there's anything in it. You'll have to report on me to Mum, you know.'

Unusually, Megan wasn't ready with an opinion. She

seemed preoccupied. 'What do you read in his face?' she asked.

Delyth was instantly wary. Her sister was good at faces. She was knowing rather than tactful. Once she had sculpted the head of a politician in bronze. The politician had loved it, but a reviewer had pointed out that it showed every flaw in the man's character. 'I don't know,' she said. 'What do you read in his face?'

As Delyth had known, Megan wasn't having this. 'I asked first. Tell me about his character.'

'I've really only known him a few days. He'll be one of the bosses I'll be working with most regularly for the next six months. He's very competent and I think I'll learn a lot from him. He works fast and hard and expects everyone else to do the same.'

'I'll bet he works hard,' Megan said. 'Go on, tell me about his face.'

'He's fit,' Delyth went on. 'I never see him still for long. His face is pleasant, not traditionally good-looking but all right. Nice curved mouth and good teeth but doesn't smile much.' She hesitated. 'He...attracts me more than any man I've ever met.' There. She had said it.

'What about his eyes?' Megan asked, ignoring Delyth's confession.

'Well, they're grey, I suppose, but—'

'Haven't you ever heard that the eyes are the windows of the soul?' Megan asked impatiently. 'You're sounding like a doctor, not a woman. What do his eyes tell you?'

'I'm both doctor and woman,' Delyth said sturdily, 'and happy to be both. Now, you tell me about his eyes.'

'You're working too hard,' Megan muttered. 'I suppose I can't blame you, it's a family trait—we're all single-minded.'

Delyth eyed her sister with some irritation. 'You're getting annoying,' she said. 'Come on, say what you have to.'

'There's something hidden in his face. It's very interesting. I'd love to do a bust of him. But there's something he's not telling people. He goes to a lot of trouble to hide it, but it's there.'

'You can't tell all that just from looking at his face,' Delyth said. 'You're making it up.'

'I've done it before,' Megan said flatly, 'and I've been right, haven't I?'

Delyth thought a minute. 'Yes,' she said.

She went back to her room at the residence, worked for a while and then slept for a couple of hours. She was learning to sleep whenever she could. Often there wasn't the chance.

For a small treat she allowed herself time for long, luxurious preparations. She had a scented bath instead of a shower, rinsed her hair and sat in her room for the long process of drying it. While she did so she listened to the *Messiah* on her CD player, singing along with the contralto part—indeed, all the parts.

It wasn't hard to decide on a dress—she didn't have all that many. She decided she'd wear— The phone rang.

'I liked your sister,' the instantly recognisable voice said, 'and I'm looking forward to the party.'

She'd only known him for a few days. He was a colleague and becoming a friend, but was it normal to feel such a burst of pleasure at hearing his voice unexpectedly? James?' she asked.

'I'm causing trouble, as ever, because I left before making those social sounds that are so important. It's every woman's question. What shall I wear?'

She giggled. 'All women have a different answer to that.'

'Well, I've got my penguin suit, but I don't think it will be that formal. I've got the clerical grey interview suit too, but I doubt that is the right thing. I'm lost.'

She told him, 'Megan has a wide variety of friends and

some of them will be wearing suits. Others will be in jean You'll just have to decide.'

She heard him sniff. 'If you gave me that kind of briefin on the ward I'd give you a real telling-off. You're suppose to make my life easy. What're you going to wear?'

Time to make her mind up. 'I've got a dark blue dress

'Right. Grey goes with blue. I'll wear a light grey su Should I bring a bottle?'

'Doubt if it'll be that kind of party. But you could tak a bunch of flowers if you like.'

'Or descend from a helicopter with a box of chocolate You know, social life in Africa was much simpler. Shall knock on your door about half past eight?'

This was unexpected. She could meet him downstai but... 'Fine,' she said. 'I'll be ready.'

'I'll order a taxi.'

She'd made her mind up the moment he'd asked. She wear the blue dress. Now she took it from her wardrobe an looked at it dubiously. It certainly suited her. It was just th it...attracted attention.

Her hair was brushed till it shone, then she tied it bac with a blue scrunchie. She rummaged through her unde wear drawer. With this dress she couldn't wear her custom ary sensible things. She pulled on a pair of white silk Frenc knickers—she didn't want the lines of leg elastic showin through. For a moment she considered going without a br but knew it wasn't a good idea. Her breasts were high an firm but... She put on a flesh-coloured bra which contain rather than supported. It was still summer—she wasn't g ing to wear tights.

He'd be here in fifteen minutes. She slipped into the dres zipped it up and looked at herself. It was of blue silk, high necked at the front but with a V-back and sleeveless. The was a slash to the right thigh. Her sister Bethan had boug it for her as a twenty-first birthday present. She remembered when she had first shown it, it had silenced all the family. 'Only a young girl could wear a dress like that,' her mother had said.

The skirt was lined, but even so it clung to her body like a second skin. She brushed it down, sat again and put on just a little more than her usual minimal make-up. Her green eyes were a good feature—she'd emphasise them a bit more.

Finally, she was finished. The 'Hallelujah Chorus' roared out of her CD player. She smiled and joined in. There was a knock at the door.

James looked well in a light grey suit. With it he wore a darker grey shirt and a tie in dull rich colours—maroon, amber, navy. And his expression was startled.

'Delyth, you look...' He swallowed. 'You look wonderful.'

'I *can* dress up when I want,' she pointed out. 'I don't spend all my time in flat shoes and sensible clothes to go with a doctor's white coat.'

'But your hair! It's right down your back. I'd no idea it was so long. It's glorious.'

She felt pleased at the compliment. 'Thank you. It's my one feminine concession. The rest of my life is concentrating on being a good doctor—this is my bit of wildness. But it can get in the way. Sometimes I think I'll cut it off.'

'Don't! It would be a tragedy.'

She decided to change the subject. 'Anyway, you've made an effort, too. I've never seen you look so—debonair.'

'What a lovely word. Remind me to look it up.'

Stepping back from the door, she waved him in. 'Come in. There's not a lot of room but you can sit on the bed.'

He came in, sat as directed and looked round. 'Why did I know your room would be like this?' he asked. 'All it is is a box, and yet you've turned it into a home. I've got a

hospital flat round the corner. Take the clothes and books
out of it and there'd be nothing of me left.'

'You need a good woman,' she said, then blushed. 'Sorry
didn't mean that.'

He smiled at her ferociously. 'One day I'll quote that back
to you.'

She thought it would be a good idea to change the subject
'What's that in your hand?' she asked. It was a small box
wrapped in dark red paper.

He shrugged. 'I'm not taking a bottle or flowers. It's just
a little gift for my hostess.'

'What is it? I've got an enquiring mind.'

'You're just nosy,' he told her. 'Wait and see.'

As it was Saturday night, those in the residence who weren't
working were certainly going out. The entire building
seemed to be full of bodies, rushing to the bathroom, ironing
clothes, demanding to borrow scent or shoes. They were
bound to be noticed. Delyth had thought of this. Once she
would have asked him to meet her in the quad or even on
a street corner. Now she was happy to have him call for
her. She knew hospital gossip was like wildfire. So what?
Never before in her medical career had she caused any kind
of interest. She could do so now.

Crouch End was an interesting district. Their taxi took
them up the steep hill so all of London lay displayed below
them. Delyth liked the variety of restaurants and the walk
along the old railway route to Highgate. The taxi drew up
at a large Victorian house, converted into four flats. She
explained that Megan had a flat, as well as a studio at the
back of the house which had been converted from the old
coach houses.

'I should have asked,' James said. 'I saw Megan wasn't
wearing a wedding ring so I presume she's not married
Does she have what is usually called a partner?'

'Not at the moment,' Delyth said, 'though she has had several.' She knew she sounded both defensive and rather prudish.

He spotted it. 'I take it that you don't approve?'

'Megan is entitled to live her own life. She seems to have a man for a year or so and then turns him in for another one. Usually she stays friends, though.'

'You disapprove of that?'

She was slightly irritated. 'It's not my business. It certainly isn't yours. I'll just say it wouldn't suit me.'

'No,' he said softly, 'I would have guessed that.' Delyth pressed the entry bell.

Megan was still in black. With a suppressed grin Delyth remembered her mother saying that a week with Megan was like staying in a funeral parlour. But, as ever, she looked striking. She was wearing a long velvet dress that caressed her figure, more opulent than Delyth's. Her jewellery was silver again, a chain belt and broad necklace with studs of jet. 'Good to see you both,' she said. 'James, I'm glad you came.'

He offered her the parcel. 'I brought you a little bread-and-butter present,' he said. 'I'm trying to ensure that I get invited back.'

'I love surprises,' Megan squeaked. 'I'm going to open it now.' She eased off the rich paper. Delyth, who was just as intrigued, noticed the care with which it had been wrapped. James's surgeon skills, no doubt.

Eventually Megan pulled off the last sheet of tissue paper and the sisters looked at what was inside. It was a carving in dark stone of— Was it a man's face? Whatever it was, it was ugly, Delyth thought. She looked at her sister and realised Megan was entranced. 'This is for me?' Megan asked, her voice low. 'It's lovely but you can't give it away.'

'I can,' he said. 'It was given to me by someone who valued it, and I'm pleased to give it to someone else who

will also value it. I don't like collecting things—it's jus
been lying in a drawer.'

'It's beautiful. James, are you sure?'

'Certain. I don't want it. I suspect Delyth thinks it'
ugly—I could tell by what you were looking at this mornin₉
that you'd like it.'

'I'm going to show it to people,' Megan announced
'Come and meet a few.'

Megan's parties were always fun. Her mother had once sai₵
that Megan collected friends with the same care as mos
people picked furniture. There was a large living roo
opening out onto an open balcony—just enough space to le
twenty-odd people eddy about, talking and drinking. Delyt
didn't stay with James all the time. Everyone here was s₵
friendly, she felt she didn't need to. For a while she chatte₵
to a man who introduced himself as Charles Kay, a barriste
who lived in one of the other flats in the house. Then sh₵
found herself refereeing an argument between two friend:
both in checked open-necked shirts, about the relative merit:
of *Eastenders* and *Coronation Street*. Then James fetche₵
her to defend Wales as a holiday destination rather tha
Scotland. It was that kind of party.

She drank spritzers, and watched approvingly as Jame:
drank beer sparingly. She noticed he was a success at th₵
party, being able to be pleasant without being obtrusive. Th₵
more she saw of him, the more she liked him. For a while
she thought, he was less driven, more relaxed.

The party was still going strong when she walked wit
Megan down to the front door to say goodbye to one of th₵
guests who had to leave early. His name was Jennett, an₵
he was a portrait painter.

'You should do a bronze of your sister,' he told Megan
'She has a glorious Celtic face.'

'Like to but I can't,' Megan said briefly. 'She's too close to me. I couldn't distance myself.'

This made no sense to Delyth, but Jennett seemed to understand. 'I see,' he said sadly. 'A pity, though.'

'I'm really enjoying myself,' Delyth said as she climbed back up the stairs. 'And I think James—'

It had never happened so quickly before. A rush of pain and horror. The sudden realisation was so unexpected that she had to hang onto the bannister, scared she might fall. It was like sharing someone's pain. She leaned there, white-faced, trying to grasp what had happened.

'Delyth! Are you all right?' Megan rushed back to her and eased her till she was sitting on the stairs, then put an arm round her. 'Are you feeling ill? Anything you've eaten or drunk?'

It wasn't that kind of pain. She shook her head. 'I just feel a bit faint. I'll be all right in a minute.'

Megan leaned her against the wall. 'What you need is a doctor. Good thing we've got one.' She ran to her flat door, ignoring Delyth's feeble protests. A minute later she reappeared with James.

He knelt in front of her. In spite of his obvious concern, he was the efficient doctor, taking her pulse and feeling her forehead. 'A bit erratic but nothing much to worry about,' he said after a while. 'What exactly happened, Delyth? Did you run up the stairs too quickly?'

It was nothing like that. And the knowledge hit her again. She wasn't in pain—it was someone else. 'Who lives in that flat?' she asked Megan, pointing to the door on the other side of the landing.

Megan looked puzzled. 'Why, it's Charles Kay—you were talking to him before. He left earlier—he's got an important case starting on Monday and needs to look through his brief. Why?'

'Someone in that flat is dangerously ill,' Delyth said. 'Dying even.'

Megan shook her head. 'Charles lives alone. And you saw him. He's in excellent health.'

'If he's alone then he's dying, I tell you.'

Now it was James's turn to be serious and concerned. 'Can you give us any good reason why you think that, Delyth?'

She couldn't. She knew they thought her foolish, and perhaps she was. Maybe she should just forget about it, rejoin the party and have another drink. And the minute she considered it, the certainty was there again, stronger than ever. Somebody needed help. 'We need to talk to him,' she persisted.

She didn't like the way James was looking at her, as if she were a hysterical girl. He was just being accommodating because she was being stupid. The thought irritated her. 'Can we at least ring his doorbell?' she said. 'He won't have gone to bed yet.'

'He won't like being disturbed,' Megan muttered. 'But if you have to…'

There was no answer to their ring, or to the second and third. 'I'll go in the flat and phone him,' Megan said. 'He may be in his study.'

James and Delyth stayed outside. Delyth kept her eyes fixed on the floor, but she couldn't remain silent and eventually she asked, 'You think I'm being stupid, don't you?'

His reply was calm, reasonable. 'I think you may be wrong, Delyth. But stupid is the last thing I would ever call you.'

His very reasonableness irritated her. 'We'll just have to wait and see, won't we?' she snapped. After that they both remained silent.

Megan reappeared. 'It's ringing but there's no reply,' she said. 'And I'm certain he's in. D'you think he could be in the bath or something?'

'He's not in the bath,' Delyth said flatly.

Unhappily, Megan produced a key. 'We each have a key to the other's flat. In case of a flood or something. But I've never been in without an invitation. If we go barging in and he's working or something, then he's not going to be well pleased.'

It was James who answered. 'Ring for the last time. If there's no answer, we'll let ourselves in. If we look fools, then so be it.'

There was no reply to their ringing. James took the key and opened the door. 'Charles...are you there?' Megan called. There was still no answer. The three entered a hall with the light still on, and walked forward. The door was opened to one room, and they peered in. It was a study. Delyth caught a glimpse of an antique desk, book-lined walls. But on the floor was a figure, in shirt and trousers, with blood in a pool round the head.

As Megan cowered into the background, James and Delyth knelt at each side of Charles. James felt the neck and nodded at Delyth. 'He's breathing and he's got a pulse, weak and irregular but it's there. Can we take a look at that cut? Megan, there's a phone there. Ring 999 for an ambulance.'

Delyth sprang to her feet, found the kitchen and took a damp clean cloth. Carefully she wiped away the blood from the injured head. There was a clean cut there, long but not deep. She compressed the cloth over it.

'Head wounds bleed a lot,' James muttered, 'but I doubt this is enough to cause unconsciousness. 'Breathing very shallow...'

She looked round. 'There's blood on the corner of the desk, James. He could have caught his head as he fell. But why did he—?'

They both guessed at once. 'Heart attack,' James said. He's still breathing but he could arrest at any minute.

Megan, fetch a couple of pillows, will you? If we have him in a semi-recumbent position it will ease the strain on his heart.'

Megan did as requested, and Delyth and James eased Charles over and slid the pillows under his head and shoulders. Is…he going to be all right?' Megan asked.

'We need to get him to hospital where they have the proper equipment,' James said. 'The paramedics will have some of it. Otherwise, we just sit here and hope he doesn' arrest. If he does, then it's mouth-to-mouth and external heart massage.'

'I'll go down to meet the ambulance,' Megan said. 'Did you know there's still a party going on in my flat?'

James was unusually silent in the taxi going home. The party had broken up when the ambulance arrived. Megan had gone to hospital with Charles and would try to get in touch with his relations. Delyth couldn't work out James' mood. He seemed irritated, almost angry. She decided to say nothing.

'We've got a problem, Delyth,' he said when they finally stepped out of the taxi. 'I suspect you saved that man's life.

'*We* saved his life,' she corrected him. 'And, if anything, the paramedics did most.' As ever, the green-coated figures had efficiently taken charge at once. 'Why, what's the problem?'

They stood facing each other in the quad, the lights of St Helen's all around them. When he didn't answer at once she said, 'The party finished in rather a hurry. Would you like to come to my room for a coffee and we can talk?'

'Yes,' he said, 'I would like that.'

He sat on her bed, took off his coat and loosened his tie. She went to switch on the percolator in the kitchen then changed from her blue dress into a tracksuit in the bathroom

When they both were clutching mugs of coffee, she asked, 'What's the matter, James?'

He had obviously thought out what he was going to say. 'You're going to tell me that some mysterious sixth sense told you that Charles Kay was ill. You knew because you are the seventh child of a seventh child—or some such mumbo-jumbo.'

'I didn't say it was because I was a seventh child,' she protested. 'I told you that almost as a joke.' She felt like fighting back. 'Anyway, if it wasn't a sixth sense, how did I know?'

'Good point,' he conceded grudgingly, 'but still quite answerable. Like I said before, you're a trained doctor—you've learned more than you realise. When you talked to the man earlier you subconsciously recognised the signs of an incipient heart attack. I'm impressed. But it's got nothing to do with the supernatural. Just admit it, Delyth!'

She thought a while. 'You're angry again,' she said, 'and I don't know why. It's not just that I'm being unscientific, it's more than that. Please tell me what it is.'

There was a long pause, so long that she thought he wasn't going to answer. Then he said, 'I'm an orphan. My parents were in a car crash when I was two. When I was eighteen I felt I had to know what happened so I looked up what had happened. I checked in newspapers, hospital records, family papers. My father was killed at once. My mother was badly injured, but she survived.'

He drank from his mug. Delyth kept silent. When he spoke his voice was thick. 'In hospital my mother came under the influence of a faith healer. In spite of all good advice, she was persuaded to sign herself out of hospital. Three weeks later she was back in again, and she died the next day. Technical cause of death, pneumonia. Real cause of death, neglect. Instead of antibiotics, this self-styled healer had been burning leaves under her nose. She said she had divined the spiritual cause of the sickness. I looked her up. She died of drink eight years later.'

Delyth put her hand on his arm. 'I'm so sorry,' she said. 'My family means everything to me. I just can't imagine being without one.'

'Being without a family has its good points. It means no one has a call on you.'

It seemed a sad note on which to end a wonderful day.

CHAPTER THREE

ON SUNDAY morning Delyth had the rarest of pleasures, an extra two hours in bed. She sat there, reading, feeling suitably decadent. Then Megan rang her.

'Charles is out of danger and very grateful. I've located his sister—she's coming down from the Midlands this afternoon. I must say, youngest sister, you make my parties more exciting than I really like.'

'Just luck we were there,' Delyth said cautiously.

'Good luck for Charles. I don't understand it. Do people have massive heart attacks without warning? I thought you usually had little ones first.'

'It can happen that way. But ischaemic heart disease kills a lot of people and it can strike anyone at almost any age. Charles will probably have to alter his lifestyle.'

Megan was dubious. 'Hmm. He won't like that.' She decided to change the subject. 'How serious are you about James? You've only just met him and yet you seem to be seeing a lot of him. I know you. You've never had much time for men before—why pick on this one?'

'I think he's special,' Delyth said simply.

'He's special all right. And that carving he gave me is wonderful—I don't know how he could bear to part with it. I like him, but I don't know if he's the one for you.'

'Something about his face?' Delyth asked sardonically. 'Something you can see that I can't?'

'Perhaps I'm wrong. I hope so. Keep in touch.' Megan rang off.

In her dressing-gown Delyth padded down the corridor to make herself some tea, then sat in bed again and thought.

Unusually for her, she hadn't thought much about herself and James. She had been content to let things develop as they would. She realised she had felt a blithe confidence that everything would be all right. Compared with the agonising she had gone through with previous boyfriends, that was amazing.

She wasn't stupid. She knew she was attractive to men. She liked the company of men—got on well with Matt, for example. While training she had had a number of boyfriends, but there had never been one whom she'd thought could have been the only man for her. She had liked them, felt comfortable with them, even admired a couple. But she'd never felt she could really love any of them. With a shock, she realised that James could be different. She had felt the attraction the first time they'd met. Since then every meeting had made her more and more certain.

Why was that such an unsettling thought? She didn't really know how he felt about her. Certainly he liked her, but did he feel the same about her as she felt about him? Just for a moment she had some idea of what people meant when they said that love hurt. It had never hurt in the past. The worst she had felt when parting from someone had been a mild regret. But with James her life was going to change.

It would be polite to let him know how Charles was. She knew he was on the ward so she phoned and left a nonurgent message that Charles was all right. An hour later he phoned back—as she had secretly hoped he would.

'I'm pleased about Charles,' he said, 'and I enjoyed the party and meeting Megan. Are there really another five like you two?'

'I'm afraid so. And my mother as well. You must meet them all some time.'

'I'd like that— Oh, excuse me a minute.' Delyth could hear the rumble of conversation. Someone had thought something important enough to interrupt him.

'Sorry about that,' he said when he came back. 'We're busy here. Look, I've got a meeting at another hospital to-night, but can we have another late drink in the Clubroom tomorrow night? Say the last half-hour?'

She thought rapidly. 'Love to, but it'll have to be late. I'm going to listen to some jazz again. I wouldn't normally, but I used to know the band from home.'

'From home? A Welsh jazz band?' His voice was comi-cally disbelieving.

'The Welsh are a musical race,' she said, mock-primly. 'All sorts of music, too.'

'I believe you. If you're seeing friends, would you like to put our drink off till another night?'

'No. I'd much rather have a drink with you,' she said. Then she sat, appalled at her own honesty.

'Half ten tomorrow night, then.' Behind him, she could hear the sound of another voice. 'Must go, Delyth.'

I hope he doesn't think I'm one of those young doctors who throws herself at the senior staff, she thought as she replaced the receiver. Then she decided that she was certain that he didn't.

'Birdie Jones is talking about signing himself out,' an anx-ious young junior nurse told Delyth next morning. 'Says he's fed up with lying still in hospital and wants to get out again.'

Delyth looked up from the pile of reports she was filling in, and frowned. This was a not unusual problem. Patients had the right, of course, to take themselves out of hospital at any time that suited them. Most accepted the doctors' advice as to the best time to leave, but some—particularly drug addicts—just had to get back on the streets. Usually they came back a few weeks later in a much worse state. But she didn't think Birdie was a junkie. 'Any special rea-son he wants to leave?' she asked.

'He says he's got things to do. But he won't say what.'

'I'll come and have a word with him,' Delyth decided. 'He's just not capable of living on his own at present.'

But Birdie thought otherwise. 'You can't keep me here if I don't want to stay,' he said belligerently. 'I'll come to have my dressings changed in the clinic. You can have the bed for some poor devil who needs it.'

'You're the poor devil who needs it,' she told him. 'Birdie, don't you realise how close you were to dying? And you're still very weak. You need the hospital rest.'

She saw the sudden flash of fear cross his face, quickly replaced by his usual impassive stare. 'I've got my own reasons for wanting to get out,' he said.

It was the first indication he'd given that there was some special reason for his wish to leave. Delyth seized her advantage. 'Come on, tell me. It's not your family, is it? You said you'd lost touch with them.'

'I have. But it's sort of family.' Birdie, the streetwise hard man, looked embarrassed. 'It's my dog. He's called Reginald.'

'Reginald?' asked Delyth, managing to keep a straight face.

'I had to call him something. Anyway, we usually sleep in that underpass near Marble Arch. He won't mind too much if I'm missing for a while and he'll hang around there for a day or two, and one or two of me mates will give him the odd scrap. But if I'm gone for long he might leave for good.'

'There's nowhere he can stay in the hospital,' she said.

'I know. That's why I've got to get out.'

'You'll kill yourself. Just lie there and let me think a bit. There must be some kind of solution.' This is a funny kind of a medical problem, she thought.

Half an hour later she thought she perhaps had a solution.

She went back to Birdie's bedside. 'How often does Reginald get fed?' she asked.

Birdie shrugged. 'He gets half of what I get. But it's not much of a feast usually.'

'I know dogs. Would he stay near the underpass if he was fed regularly?'

'Wouldn't he just? But how—?'

'If I gave him some money, would one of your mates feed the dog every day?'

'Andy would. But I haven't got—'

'I'll lend you some money. I'll take it to Andy and he can buy stuff for Reginald. Can I trust Andy with the money?'

'If it's for the dog, 'course you can,' Birdie said indignantly. 'He's got a dog of his own, he knows what it's like. But why should you lend me money? I'm just a rough sleeper, a beggar.'

She shrugged. 'It's for your dog. I think you'll pay me back.'

He looked at her in silence. 'I will,' he said. 'It might take time but I will.'

In her lunchbreak Delyth took a taxi to Marble Arch and walked into the complex of tunnels underneath. Andy was sitting on the floor where Birdie had said he'd be, a bearded, long-haired figure in an ex-army greatcoat, his arm round an equally scruffy dog. A surprisingly intelligent eye looked at her when she asked his name.

She explained who she was, where Birdie was and how worried he was about Reginald. Then she offered the figure three five-pound notes. 'Ten pounds for dog food,' she said, 'and a further five pounds for yourself.'

Andy took ten pounds and offered her five back. In a cultured voice he said, 'Thank you for looking after Birdie and bothering to come down here. I'll happily take the money for Reginald. But on this occasion there's no need to give me anything.'

She pushed the note back to him. 'Then buy something for your dog. Bye, Andy.'

She caught a taxi back to work. The entire trip had taken only twenty minutes, and when she reported to Birdie he looked much happier.

Many people in hospital, she knew, would think that she'd acted foolishly. Her job was to treat people for illnesses, not act as a social worker. But she felt good.

Then, as she left Birdie's little side-ward, a nurse said, 'Could you have a word with Mrs Webster? She's had nothing to eat today. She's a bit…upset.'

The oncology registrar had been to see Mrs Webster. The results of the mammogram and fine needle biopsy had only confirmed what everyone had already guessed—the lump was malignant. Now Mrs Webster was scheduled for a lumpectomy and then radiotherapy.

Giving news like this, it was always difficult. The registrar had explained things as carefully as possible, and had made himself available for further explanations when Mrs Webster came in to visit that evening. At first it seemed that Wendy had accepted her bad news with resignation, but it now turned out that the resignation had been incomprehension. She just could not come to terms with having cancer

When Delyth entered her little room Wendy raised a tear-blotched face from her pillow. 'What d'you want?' she asked. 'Not more examinations. I've had enough.'

Delyth was getting used to aggression. It wasn't an uncommon reaction to bad news. Sitting on the bed, she said gently, 'I've just come to see if you're all right, Wendy Why haven't you eaten anything today?'

'What's the point of eating if I'm going to die anyway I only came in here to have my legs done. If I'd known this was going to happen I wouldn't have come.'

'Nobody says you're going to die,' Delyth said carefully. 'Certainly, you're more ill than you thought, but we've caught things early. I should be optimistic if I were you.'

'You're not me! You're not married. What'll Harry do if I die?'

'There's no need to talk of dying. Now, you need to keep your strength up. Can I get you a sandwich or something?'

'I thought you said I was overweight. Why are you trying to feed me?'

And so it went on. Delyth knew that Wendy was incapable of reasonable argument. Her fear was beyond logic. For a while she considered prescribing a beta-blocker, a pill to lower anxiety, but decided against it. Eventually, perhaps soothed by the constant reassurance, Wendy grew calmer. 'I'll get a nurse to fetch you something to eat,' Delyth said, making her escape. 'You'll feel better then.'

She felt drained by the short interview. Medicine isn't just drugs, she told herself.

By evening she was looking forward to her evening of listening to jazz. She arrived early at the pub and asked to go to the tiny room where the band was unpacking. She knew they'd be busy. For an amateur group there was often more work backstage than on-stage. Their leader, Alex Llewellyn, was pleased to meet an old friend, as were the others. At one stage she had seen a lot of the band, but inevitably their paths had divided.

'Where's Meriel?' she asked, referring to the band's singer.

'She's left us. Earning large sums of money, doing something with computers. Now we're working we don't get together as often as we used to.' It was the usual fate of student bands, even the good ones. 'Going to stay behind for a bit of a party afterwards?' Alex asked.

'Can't,' she said. 'Tomorrow I must work.' It had been fun, being a student.

When the band went on stage she sat with Matt and the others, who were regular attendees at the live jazz nights. Matt offered her a drink. She asked for ginger beer and ice.

'Heard you went out with James Owen on Saturday night,' he said, elaborately casually.

'I took him to a party at my sister's.' There was no keeping anything quiet in a hospital. Not that she particularly wanted to keep her relationship quiet. And James didn't seem to mind.

'Lucky James,' Matt said, but she thought he didn't mean it unpleasantly.

They listened to the band play. This wasn't a traditional band like the one which had played last time. It was quieter, with a line-up of bass, drums, keyboard and guitar. But they were skilful musicians, and she enjoyed the playing. Matt and his pals weren't quite so keen, although they listened and applauded politely. In the intervals between the numbers they talked about football. Delyth winced.

'I asked,' a voice said. 'Ginger beer and ice. I'm even going to try one myself.'

She looked up. There was James, two drinks in his hands. It was just because it was unexpected, that was all, but her heart gave a mighty thump, she felt her mouth go dry and she couldn't at once reply.

Casual again, he was dressed in jeans and a light blue T-shirt. The lights were lowered in the pub, but the power of her eyesight seemed more intense. She could see the wisps of hair on his forearms. She noticed the way the T-shirt creased as it tucked into the flat waist of his jeans, even the mobile phone attached to his belt.

She thought she must look foolish, sitting there unable to speak, mouth half-open. It was less than forty-eight hours since she had last seen him yet she was struck dumb by

im. He was growing on her; the face she'd thought not
eally handsome now had a tremendous attraction. He
miled. 'Room for a little one?'

She slid sideways to let him in. He sat, and nodded to
he others, telling them that he'd enjoyed it so much last
me that he couldn't keep away. They smiled and nodded
ack, but Delyth saw the sudden sharp glance Matt directed
t her.

She managed to speak. 'I'm not supposed to see you till
alf past ten,' she said, and instantly felt annoyed with her
lumsy remark. She was twenty-four years old, a doctor,
nd she was still acting like a young teenager on her first
ate.

'Sorry,' he said urbanely, 'but I got fed up with work and
remembered how much I enjoyed myself here last time.
ou don't mind me coming, do you?'

'Of course not! It's open to anyone, isn't it? I didn't mean
at. We're pleased to see you and...'

He laid his hand on her arm, and his touch thrilled her.
aughing, he said, 'I'm very glad to be here. Now let's
sten.'

Fortunately the band struck up again. She needed a few
inutes to calm herself. Alex and his friends were playing
clever arrangement of 'Sweet Georgia Brown', and she
njoyed the jazz classic. When they'd finished she clapped
ith the others, having regained her composure. 'I *am* glad
ou've come,' she said more calmly. 'You should enjoy
lex's music.'

'I came to be with you,' he replied. 'The music is just an
xtra.' And she felt flustered again. 'Are we still having that
st drink in the Clubhouse?' he went on.

She didn't hesitate. 'Yes,' she said firmly. 'I'm looking
orward to it.'

After that the conversation became more general, James
aking part in a heated argument about medical politics.

Should there be a vast increase in the number of consult
ants? Delyth noticed with some amusement that Matt and
the other two were conservatives, saying that the number
were about right, and James was arguing for expansion. A
ever, James argued vehemently but not overbearingly
Delyth was almost sorry when the band started again.

She was enjoying herself. There were five of them on the
banquette, now pushed together. She was aware of the
warmth of James, the feeling of his bare arm against hers
the length of his muscled thigh pressing through the thinnes
of her skirt. It was…exciting.

The band finished to more enthusiastic applause. Ale
thanked everybody, said how much they liked playing here
and how they were always made welcome. 'A lot of people
have asked about Meriel, our singer,' he went on. 'Well
sadly, she's now making her fortune in computers. Bu
there's someone here who's sung with us in the past and
we'd like to ask her to join us now for just one song before
the interval. Delyth Price!'

For the second time that evening Delyth was shocked
She shouldn't have been—this had happened before. She
didn't stand at once, and a grinning band member swung a
spotlight on her. People turned to look.

Beside her James was bemused. 'You can sing?' he mut
tered.

Led by the band, the applause grew louder. 'Oh, I can
sing all right,' she whispered, and stood to walk to the band
She wasn't nervous. She knew she could sing in public.

'You might have warned me,' she grumbled to Alex a
she climbed onto the dais.

He smiled. 'You should sing more than you do. And lot
of people asked for Meriel and I knew you were just a
good. What can you remember?'

She had already decided. 'I want to sing ''Summertime''.

'That's great. Let's go.'

She was confident in the introduction and knew she'd fit in well with the band. She'd sung this with them before. Unconsciously she clasped her hands, the way she always did when singing, waited for her moment and started on the long, drawn-out first notes. It wasn't an easy song, but it was an effective one. She was happy in the spotlight, for a moment in the career she could have taken up instead of medicine.

When she finished the applause was louder than it had been all evening, and there were calls for an encore, but Alex wouldn't put on her. The house lights came up and he said firmly they would be back after the interval. Delyth walked back to rejoin her friends, smiling at people who clapped her as she passed. She had forgotten the buzz she used to get from performing. Now she was rather smugly aware of the shock she had caused James, Matt and his friends.

James was smiling but silent, the others rather boisterous in their congratulations. When she sat by him he whispered, 'Delyth, that was wonderful. How many more ways are you going to amaze me?'

'There's a lot to me you don't know,' she said cheerfully. 'I used to sing an awful lot.' Now thoroughly confident, she looked at her watch. 'It's a quarter past ten. D'you still want to go to the Clubhouse?'

He looked startled. 'Yes. But don't you want to stay longer?'

'I decided earlier that I'd leave now. Shall we go?'

They left, James somehow making it obvious to the others that they weren't invited. Delyth saw Matt looking glum, and hoped she wasn't going to have trouble with him. She did quite like him.

By now she was used to James's rapid pace through the streets. He was silent as they first walked so she commented, 'You're quiet.'

'I was thinking of your singing. Why didn't you tell me you had such a glorious voice?'

She felt happy at the compliment. 'It never came up,' she pointed out. 'I can't just say out of the blue, ''I've got a glorious voice.'' And it doesn't have much to do with medicine.'

'You're good enough to be a professional,' he said abruptly. 'Did you never think of it?'

'Just a bit. My family were very keen—they're all something artistic except me. I'm the unusual one. My sisters think I'm odd. But I always knew that I was going to be a doctor. I didn't even worry that I wouldn't get the grades— I just knew I would.'

'Hmm. I'm only just realising how little I know about you.'

'How could you?' she asked. 'We only met five days ago.'

He looked startled. 'Good Lord, you're right. But it feels...like ages.' He took her hand, and she squeezed his. 'This isn't like me,' he said.

'I know. Everyone I've talked to in hospital is a little bit frightened of you. They say you're a very good doctor but you're driven—you don't like mistakes. They hate it when you frown at them.'

'Thank you for that comprehensive character assassination,' he said drily. 'Are you afraid of me, Delyth?'

They had just reached the Saracen's Head. She entered and walked down the passage to the Clubroom like a regular. His question was an interesting one, she realised. 'No, I'm not afraid of you,' she said slowly. 'And I know I ought to be. I was terrified when I was in my last year of training and the prof. told me off. Even though he did it like a gentleman. Usually I'm very much in awe of those in authority. Why don't you frighten me?'

'I must be slipping,' he told her. 'I used to terrify young
use officers.'

They entered the Clubroom; she recognised quite a few
ople there. In a corner there was a group of slightly older
rses, obviously celebrating a birthday or something, who
re getting rather noisily drunk. They waved to James, and
waved back cheerfully. 'Come and join us!' a nurse of
out forty with a rather hard face shouted.

James shook his head. 'We're not here to enjoy ourselves.
lyth and I have business to talk over.'

The rest of the group seemed happy with this, but the
rse who had called looked sour. 'Suit yourself,' she said.

'You're a quick liar,' Delyth whispered to him as they
down. 'You just didn't want to go over there, did you?'

'Nothing worse than being sober when all around you
n't. We'll sit here quietly and I'll fetch us more ginger
er.' He left her to go to the hatch, and just for a moment
e was aware of the malevolent stare of the hard-faced
rse. Why?

They sipped their chilled soft drinks. There was some-
ng she felt she had to tell him. 'You were asking why I
n't feel frightened of you. And I can see that you're a
ghtening man. For some reason I feel all right with you.
d, James, I'm not usually a forward young woman. It's
t that I—'

'Don't say that you've got powers,' he said with a grin.
ou just feel the same about me as I feel about you. We're
racted. It's lovely, and I feel the world is a better place
cause of it, but basically it's pheromones. Simple animal
raction.'

She dug him viciously in the ribs with her finger. 'Don't
at me as a chemistry set. There's more to me than that.
s just that something is telling me that I'm…all right with
u. I've never felt it with any other man either.'

He looked at her thoughtfully. 'You really mean that,

don't you? Delyth, I'm a scientist like you, a rationalist
don't like mystical ideas.'

'I do mean it,' she said helplessly. 'James, I know the
ideas aren't scientific. I've tried to get rid of them, b
they're part of me.'

He put his arm round her waist. 'I still like you a lot,'
said. Somehow, that made things seem better.

The group across the room stood and noisily started
leave, the hard-faced nurse waving again. James smiled
her, but Delyth felt there was something threatening in
smile. She felt a bit sorry for the nurse. 'Have you ev
drunk too much?' she asked. 'I mean, ever found yours
drinking because you had to?'

He frowned. She didn't know why she had asked. She
expected him to say no at once. But he paused before a
swering. 'There was a time when it was a definite temp
tion. When things get on top of you it's very easy to ha
a quick Scotch, and another... Then you find yourself loc
ing forward to getting home so you can have the first.'

She was amazed at this. James always seemed so mu
in control. 'You didn't really have a problem?' she aske

He laughed. 'No. Just once I got close enough to reali
there could be a problem if I let it.'

The hard-faced nurse put her head round the door a
shouted, 'We're off now. Evening, all.' She looked direc
at James. ''Night, Angel.' Then she was dragged off by l
friends.

The two sat in silence for a moment. Then Delyth sa
'You don't usually let your emotions show, do you? You'
got a stone face—or you can have. But just for a mome
there I could see you were hurt when she called you ''A
gel''. Why?' She thought, then said, 'You don't have to t
me if you don't want to.'

She wondered if she had gone too far. He remained sile
his face impassive. Then he said absently, 'That was St

urse Bentley. I've known her vaguely for years. She'll be
orry she said that when she sobers.'

'If she remembers,' Delyth said sharply. 'She meant it to
urt.'

'True.' He emptied his glass and set it smartly back on
e table with a rap. 'Just for a minute there I was tempted
fetch myself a whisky. Silly idea. I'm on call.'

There was another pause, then he went on, 'You would
ave heard about this in time, Delyth. You can't hide any-
ing in hospital. I did intend to tell you. It's something
erhaps you should know. She called me Angel—it's short
or Angel of Death.'

'That's not very nice,' Delyth said, 'for a doctor.'

He went on emotionlessly. 'I was engaged to be married
nce—to another doctor. We trained together, her name was
rin Shaw. We'd been together since we were eighteen and
e wanted to stay together. I loved her.'

Delyth tried to ignore the ignoble shaft of jealousy that
visted inside her. 'Go on,' she said. 'What happened?'

'She died. We were both working very hard—house doc-
rs, like you now. She didn't pay enough attention to her-
lf, thought she was just tired. It's a joke, isn't it, training
be a doctor, spotting other people's illnesses and ignoring
ur own? She thought she was just run down, but she had
ukaemia. It took three months from illness to death.'

Delyth was shocked at the sheer horror of the story, at
e matter-of-fact way he told it. But then she looked at his
ak face, and knew that he was feeling it all again. 'When
as this?' she asked.

'A long time ago now, over eight years.'

She was going to say something which she knew would
e trite, something about how time would heal everything.
hey she looked at him more closely and asked, 'There's
mething else, isn't there?'

'Afraid so. It took me time to get over Erin's death. I did

it largely by working like a lunatic. But in time I did g
over it. And after a while I found another girl, Hila
Tennyson. Not a doctor, a nurse this time. She helped n
get over Erin's death—she'd known her, had nursed her.
began to enjoy life again and, in fact, we were living t
gether. Then she was hit by a runaway lorry and never r
covered consciousness. Died after three days.'

He turned to her with a savage smile. 'Going out wi
me could be dangerous, Delyth. Women I love seem to di
One of the nurses called me the Angel of Death. The nic
name stuck.'

There was nothing Delyth could say. She stared at hir
white-faced.

CHAPTER FOUR

BEING a house officer might seem never-ending, but it was always interesting. Delyth knew she was learning. Although she could always ask for advice, she had a lot to decide herself. After her two days off she had a run in which she seemed to be working more time than there was in a week. Her hours were supposed to be limited, but if the work was here it had to be done.

Frank Allison looked at her suspiciously. He was seventy, and had never come across anything like this in his life. 'It can't be natural,' he said, 'putting machines inside people and leaving them there. And you say it'll be powered by a battery? All the batteries I've ever had have run out after a month. I'm not being cut open every month.'

'These are special, very expensive batteries,' she told him. 'They last about ten years. And if you have a pacemaker fitted you'll feel a lot better. You won't be so tired and there'll be a lot less discomfort.'

'Why didn't you fit one when I came in, then? Without telling me?'

'We need to have your consent, Frank. We can't just operate on you. You have to decide whether you want the operation or not.'

Frank considered this. 'Are you absolutely certain that nothing can go wrong?'

This was a difficult question to answer, but she had been told to be absolutely honest. 'There's a risk to everything, Frank. But we can say that about one in every two thousand people has been fitted with one. And they all feel the benefit.'

'So, what exactly will you do?'

'You have it done under local anaesthetic. No need fo sending you to sleep. But we'll probably give you some thing to relax you. And it'll take no longer than an hou Afterwards you carry a card round to say you've been fitte with a pace maker, and some people wear a bracelet wit the details on.'

'I'm not wearing a bracelet! You'll be fitting me wit earrings next!'

Delyth knew the old man was being awkward on purpos obviously enjoying the conversation.

'I think you'd look sweet in earrings,' she said. 'Bi they're not necessary and the bracelet's not compulsor Now, what they do is fix a little wire in your heart and attac it to this tiny machine which we put inside your chest. Yo might be able to feel it if you touch it. But what you ce tainly will be able to feel is a lot better.'

'Not tired all the time?'

Once again she had to be careful. 'Almost certainly you' feel a lot better. But I'd be wrong if I didn't tell you th there's a tiny risk.'

'All right,' said Frank, 'where d'you want me to sign?'

Delyth took out the form for him. Before an operation a patients had to give their informed consent. 'Informed' wa the important word. It was no good just saying that an op eration was necessary. The patient had to be informed c any risks, and have a clear idea of what was involved.

Occasionally she saw James on the ward, always movin with his customary speed. He would smile at her as if the shared a secret, and she would smile back. He phoned he and said, 'I know you have no time for eating or sleepin much less washing, but how about a stolen half-hour in th Clubroom?'

After that they got into the habit of meeting there as ofte

as they could. He had to take a series of clinics in a neighbouring smaller hospital so often he didn't get back till late. He would phone, and they would snatch a few minutes together. Togetherness was all she needed, all she had time for, all she could cope with.

Their short meetings were odd. Both seemed to know that something might develop, but neither was sure what. For the moment they were busy—things would take their time.

Then, after a fortnight's hard but exciting work, she found herself with two whole days off. 'It's midweek,' she announced to him as they sat in the Clubroom, 'Wednesday and Thursday. But days are days.'

'What are you going to do? See Megan again? A bit more of London?'

'Sleep,' she said with some passion. 'Then wash my clothes, clean my room, write letters to family and friends. I might even do a little light reading.'

'All excellent ideas.' They were sitting together in the rather distant corner that had become particularly theirs. No one could overhear their conversation; people didn't come to sit with them unless invited.

'You could do all those on Wednesday,' he continued. 'How long since you had any fresh air?'

'They don't make it around here. I'm getting quite fond of diesel fumes and carbon monoxide.'

'Just as I thought. Look, I can take Thursday afternoon off. The forecast isn't bad—how about seeing the best London can do for countryside? Get out your boots and trousers and I'll pick you up at one.' He looked at her, suddenly thoughtful. 'You do walk, don't you?'

'I'm a country girl. Of course I do.'

'Good. And just for once we'll have a rule. No talk of medicine.'

'Is that possible?' she asked demurely.

'Quite possible. In fact, we'll have no depressing talk a[t] all.'

That was a coded message she recognised. He didn't wan[t] to talk about his past. When he'd told her about his tw[o] dead lovers a fortnight before, she had been too upset to as[k] for details. She remembered his account of the deaths of hi[s] parents—what a load for any man to bear! After he had tol[d] her he had taken her back to the residence and kissed he[r] gently. She had grabbed him and pulled him to her, her face next to his. She had wanted to give him comfort and sh[e] thought he had recognised this.

After a while he had put her from him, equally gently 'I'm all right really,' he had said. 'We'll talk about it som[e] time—if you want to, that is.'

'If you want to tell me,' she had answered. But since the[n] there just hadn't been time.

I'd really like a walk,' she told him.

Delyth still hadn't seen much of the centre of London, an[d] the outskirts were completely new to her. James took he[r] by train from Waterloo to Kingston-on-Thames, and they walked across the river, and along the path by its side an[d] on to Hampton Court Palace. Feeling like tourists, they wan[n]dered round, talking about history and admiring the ancien[t] buildings. But James didn't intend to saunter for long. He'[d] brought her here to walk.

They walked back through Kingston and into Richmon[d] Park. It took her a while, but she managed to get used t[o] his long, loping pace. 'I'm certainly getting my exercis[e] with you,' she panted.

'It's good for you. If more people walked further there'[d] be less work for us in hospital.'

'No talking shop,' she warned him.

It was good to feel the grass underfoot in the park. Sh[e] saw the deer and almost felt she was in the country. But i[n]

e distance she could see the great towers of the city. He
nade her walk hard so her legs ached, her lungs stretched.
hen they dropped down into Richmond and had a welcome
up of tea, sitting overlooking the river.

'I really enjoyed that,' she said. 'It was just what I
eeded. I know what you're doing—you're taking me out
f myself, reminding me there is a life outside medicine.'

He reached over the table to squeeze her hand. 'You need
remember that,' he said seriously. 'It took me a long time
realise it. Learn from my mistakes.'

'I don't think of you making mistakes.'

'Everyone makes mistakes,' he told her soberly. 'Come
n, we'll get the train back.'

It was rather fun to be on the train—there weren't too
any on it. Most people were commuting back after a day
the City, and watching the crammed trains coming the
ther way gave her a sense of escape. 'I'm quite happily
red,' she told him as their train slid into the station. 'This
as done me no end of good. But I hope our day isn't over
et.'

'Certainly not. I can either take you out to dinner or, if
ou want, you can come to my flat and I'll feed you there.'

'You're going to cook for me?'

'My domestic staff will knock something up,' he said
rbanely. 'Now, which do you want to do?'

It seemed to be a casual invitation, but she knew it wasn't.
Vhen she accepted she had the sense of making a definite
ecision, of taking a step into something new. But she ac-
epted anyway. Sometimes you had to take risks.

'I'll come to your flat,' she said, 'but I want to shower
nd change first. It'll take me about an hour.'

'Then shall I pick you up about seven?'

She shook her head. 'I wouldn't dream of it. You're close
the hospital and there are things you need to do. I'll be
nocking on your door.'

'But I'd rather—'

'Just for once let me decide. You know it makes sens
You can walk me back if you like.'

He frowned, but he agreed.

For the walk she'd had her hair in her customary Fren
plait. Now she took it down and rinsed it through in t
shower. She'd leave it long, caught back with pretty slide
She put on pretty, frilly underwear, again in white silk, th
a grey dress, cool and attractive. No tights—it was t
warm. Just a touch of make-up. She seemed to be acti
without conscious volition. What the evening would bri
she wasn't going to think about.

His flat was in a house owned by the hospital, only fi
minutes away and practically part of the complex. Thr
doctors each had a flat there. She was wondering as s
rang the bell, but a kind of faith told her that everythi
would be all right.

He answered, dressed in dark trousers and a white shi
his hair still wet. As ever, he looked wonderful. And s
knew that, as he looked at her, he found her attractive to
His eyes burned with…admiration? When she saw him,
her previous tiny doubts disappeared. She was glad she h
come.

'Delyth, come in.' He waved her through the door.
hope you're hungry. We'll dine in about half an hour. We
have a drink first.'

She'd not been to his flat before. He escorted her to
living room, pleasant enough, with cream walls and a da
ish carpet. When she sat on the couch he fetched two glass
and opened a bottle of wine. She liked the taste and t
bubbles. Then he sat beside her. She looked round a
frowned.

There was a television, a small CD player, a rack
books. Most of the books were medical tomes, dark a

heavy. 'I recognise the furniture, curtains and paint,' she told him. 'They're all hospital issue.'

He shrugged. 'I just live here. Africa was even more basic than this, and I liked that, too. It suits me—most of my time here I spend working.'

'But there's nothing of you in the room! No pictures, no photographs.'

He seemed surprised at her protestation. 'What do I want pictures of, Delyth? You don't need pictures to bring back memories. I like to travel light. If I were offered a job in America I could be ready to leave tomorrow morning. I haven't even got a car.'

She shook her head in bewilderment. 'Is it all like this? May I look round?'

'It's all like this. But look round, anyway.'

Her mother had always said that a home told you every-thing about a person's character. But this flat told her noth-ing about James. Perhaps that was the point.

There was a bedroom with lowered Venetian blinds, throwing slats of light over the double bed. There was a spare room, neatly piled with cases. A dining annexe laid for two. Everything was scrupulously neat, but it said noth-ing about the inhabitant. The flat was as bland as a hotel room.

'I don't understand you,' she said. 'You're an interesting man, an interested man. But you've got nothing. Not even books.'

'Books I can get out of the library. I don't want roots, Delyth, things to cling to me. In the end you don't own possessions—they own you.'

'Perhaps,' she muttered, 'but they show who and what you are. All this...this nothingness. It's as if you're hiding yourself.'

He didn't answer her.

The kitchen looked as if it might be used sometimes, but

that was all. The oven was on, and she stooped to peer through the glass door suspiciously. 'I'm ravenous, James. What about the meal I was promised? There's nothing in the oven. You're supposed to put food in it—it doesn't grow there.'

'Ah. I'd forgotten you were a country girl. I'll bet you are an expert cook.'

'My father has a market garden,' she said shortly. 'He grows a lot of our fresh food.'

The doorbell rang. 'Just in time,' he said cheerfully. 'I've no kitchen skills but I can certainly use a telephone.' He disappeared to open the door and returned followed by a little man, carrying a big tray. Quickly, the man stuffed foil-covered parcels into the oven or the fridge, and then disappeared.

'My good friend, Mr Hung,' said James. 'Shall we dine?'

'This is cheating,' she reproached him as they sat in the little annexe.

'Not at all. Mr Hung cooks wonderfully, I don't. On the other hand, I'm brilliant at taking out appendixes. A fair division of labour, I think. What d'you think of the menu we decided on together?'

She picked up the neatly written card Mr Hung had left on the table, and decided that this was a little more adventurous than the usual Chinese take-away. Melon with citrus fruits and blackcurrant sorbet. Cajun chicken with pepper sauce and a salad. A selection of ice creams and fresh raspberries and strawberries. 'Let's eat,' she said.

'That was a wonderful meal,' she sighed some time later. 'And I love the wine.'

He had opened another bottle—the first had seemed just to go. He had put on music, something low and seemingly distant. She recognised love songs from the Auvergne. They had decided not to bother with coffee as they still had wine. Now they sat side by side on the couch, pleasantly relaxed hands behind her head and closed her eyes. She was defenceless, offering herself to him, and it made her so happy. She heard the hiss of his breath as he gazed down at her. 'Delyth, you're beautiful,' he groaned.

There was the rustle of clothes and he was beside her, also naked. For a while he just held her, and slowly the apprehension she was feeling died away.

He kissed her more freely now she was naked. She sighed and writhed at the feeling of his lips on the side of her throat, the touch of his tongue on her nipples, now hard with desire. His hands stroked the curve of her shoulders, the delicate flatness of her stomach, the roundness of her hips.

She felt passion flowing like liquid fire through her entire body, knew that it was readying itself for that which she so intensely desired. Still with her eyes closed, she reached up to him, ran her fingertips along the leanness of his body, felt the roughness of hair, the smoothness of skin, and then heard his sudden sob of excitement as she took his hardness into her hand for a moment.

Her arms wrapped themselves round his neck, pulled him across her, down to her. Almost of their own volition her legs spread apart. She felt an infinity of excitement, of apprehension, as his body gently came down to touch hers. 'I've wanted this so much,' he muttered thickly, 'Delyth, do you know how much I've wanted you?'

'I've wanted you too,' she reproved him. 'Surely you know that? I've kept myself for you, James. Something told me this was meant to be. I know we're destined to be together for ever. It'll always be like this.'

Her happiness lasted another thirty seconds. He was poised above her. She couldn't wait any longer so she urged him down towards her, into her. 'James,' she panted.

But there was something wrong. His body, which had

been so ready, now seemed rigid with some kind of torment. He slumped to one side of her.

She opened her eyes and looked at the face next to her, now crushed into the bedding. 'James, what is it?' she asked tremulously.

His voice was now thick with some emotion other than passion. 'You said you know this is meant to be.'

'Yes…I know it. Surely you feel it, too?'

He didn't answer her question. Instead he went on, 'And you've kept yourself for me? You're a virgin?'

'I am, but it doesn't matter. James, who else should I lose my virginity to?'

Now he rolled onto his back, all bodily contact between them lost but for his hand which clutched hers. 'And you know we're destined to be together for ever. To be married, in fact… You've been told this by your voice that tells you when patients are really ill?'

Things were now dreadfully wrong. With her free hand she pulled the cover of the bed over her. She didn't want to be naked for this conversation. 'Perhaps married in time,' she faltered. 'But for now I just know we have to be together.'

He groaned. Then she felt him roll from the bed. When he spoke his voice was harsh at first, then became infinitely compassionate. But she didn't want compassion, she wanted love. 'Delyth, your voice is wrong. I'm very…fond of you. But any relationship I form will be temporary. I told you, I travel light. When I finish here I'll move on, perhaps to America—I'm already negotiating with Chicago. And I'll go alone. I've tried full-scale relationships, but they just don't work for me.'

'So you want me simply as a temporary lover?' she asked.

His reply was stark. 'Yes,' he said.

The silence between them seemed to stretch on for ever. Then she said, 'If you'd go, I'd like to get dressed.'

The thing to do was not to feel anything. She had learned on the ward that if you tried hard enough you could distance yourself from your feelings. But this was harder.

She dressed, then looked quickly round the bare bedroom. It was now nearly dark. The sun had set. She walked out of the door. He, too, had dressed, and was sitting on the couch, his expression haggard. He stood quickly.

It was the hardest thing she had ever done, but she managed to keep her voice calm, her expression neutral. 'I can't talk now, James, but I know we'll have to say something some time. But, please, not now. I'm going home and I don't want you to walk with me.'

'I've hurt you, haven't I?' he asked.

'Yes,' she said, 'you have.'

While a wee foolish of her. She wouldn't have forced work for him. Keeping positive it would be too late, she'd forced him to this tiredness. Maybe this made no less... mind way interrupted always her work, her history history process. And she'd tried... She found in her memory work, not overwhelmed...

CHAPTER FIVE

NEXT morning was dreadful. Usually when Delyth woke sh looked forward to her work, to the day. Not this time. Sh woke late, as if her subconscious had told her that wakin would bring the pain of remembrance. But somehow sh tore herself out of bed.

Since she couldn't just forget what had happened, sh forced herself to think about the night before, to decide wha she felt, what she would have to do. As she drank her earl morning cup of tea, sitting cross-legged on her bed, sh wondered if she'd ever completely get over her rejectior Not that it had really been a rejection.

Surprisingly, she didn't feel ashamed or angry at hersel She knew she had perhaps acted in a forward way, had eve led James on. But she'd done it sincerely. She thought sh had *known* James was the only man for her. The fact tha he didn't feel the same bewildered her.

She had to face the brutal fact. She had been wrong James was not for her. She muttered it aloud, 'James doesn' love me, he doesn't love me, he doesn't want me.' He dismay grew. What *could* she be certain of?

She remembered what Megan had said about James' face, about there being something hidden there. She ha been right. James had turned his back on love, on all kind of close relationships. She thought of his flat, so lacking an personal touch. What had he said? He wanted to travel ligh That was both physically and emotionally. Well, that wa his problem. She had parents, six sisters, no end of friend and relations. She knew what joy family closeness coul bring—and, for that matter, what misery.

What was she going to do? She would have to work with him, see him regularly. It took a tremendous effort, but she told herself that she would handle it. She would not let this man make her miserable. A bit of her mind, which she tried to repress, said, Not much.

It wasn't hard to lose herself in work on the ward. She found herself talking to Wendy. She had been seen by an oncologist who thought they might have caught things in time. He had scheduled her for a lumpectomy the next day, and was cautiously optimistic about the prognosis. But Wendy was one of the world's great worriers. As she talked to Delyth she felt her breast almost constantly, as if holding it gave her comfort. Her hand was always inside her nightie.

'You must show me how to feel for lumps,' she told Delyth. 'Is there anywhere else I ought to feel?'

'Your breasts are the most important place,' Delyth told her, 'though you should also check for lumps in your neck. But there are other signs to look out for. If you cough up blood, or pass it vaginally, other than in your period, you should consult your doctor. If a mole changes, or you get non-healing sores on your skin, you should be concerned. And unexplained weight loss or persistent tiredness can be an indicator, too.' She could see Wendy carefully memorising all these pointers, and for a moment felt a pang of guilt. She guessed that Wendy's GP was going to see a lot of her in the future.

'Of course,' she went on, 'those are only vague indicators. Each of them might be explained by a dozen of things other than cancer.'

'Of course, Doctor,' Wendy said. 'Now, about the operation tomorrow. They have caught it in time, haven't they? I don't really need to worry?'

Delyth sighed. She wanted to reassure her patient, but she mustn't—she couldn't—tell her that all would be certainly well. 'Well, there's always a risk,' she began carefully, 'and no operation is ever a hundred per cent successful. But with any luck you should be fine. Incidentally, we'll do your varicose veins at the same time.'

Wendy laughed. 'I'd forgotten about them,' she said.

After her patients' round there was the massive amount of paperwork to attend to—the recommendations, the requests for tests, the preparations for admission and discharge, the letters to GPs. Delyth lost herself in this, working industriously in the doctors' room, and in the middle of the afternoon James came in.

She was sitting with her back to the door and when it clicked open, somehow she knew it was him. Her body tensed. He came to stand behind her, rested his hand on her shoulder a minute, then moved it. She could feel his reluctance to take his hand away. 'Hello, James,' she said, falsely bright. 'Where have you been keeping yourself?'

He didn't respond to her cheerfulness. Instead, he came to sit opposite her at the other side of the table. 'Did you get home all right last night?'

She considered the question, and decided not to let him off the hook. 'If you mean was I mugged or molested, the answer is no.'

Softly, he said. 'No, Delyth, that's not what I meant.' He looked at her, and as she stared back into his eyes she thought they'd never been so close and yet so distant. He had on that expression she'd come to think of as his stone face. It wasn't unpleasant, but gave no indication as to what he was thinking. His eyes were impenetrable.

He said, 'I've only known you for a while but in that time I've come to have a…high regard for you. But there's been a misunderstanding, and I think it's probably my fault. You want more of me than I'm capable of giving. I want to say I'm sorry.'

She shrugged. 'Perhaps we both made mistakes. You

were very honest with me, and I don't think that a lot of men would have stopped when you did.'

The tiniest of smiles flicked across his lips. 'It wasn't easy,' he said.

'It wasn't easy for me either.' Her words were simple, and she realised they came nowhere near expressing what she really felt. Couldn't he also feel what there was—could be—between them? Apparently not. She had been so very wrong.

He went on, 'I came to tell you there's been a bit of a panic here. I was looking forward to at least working with you, and now it looks as if I can't.'

Inside her, she felt the stirrings of anger—and also of fear. 'I hope I haven't frightened you off,' she said, more viciously than she had intended. 'I do promise not to be an embarrassment to you.'

For a moment she saw anger flare in his eyes, and wondered if she had gone too far. She knew what depths of feeling he was capable of. But the anger died and he shook his head. 'Nothing to do with you, Delyth. Vic Adams, the S.R. at Lathom Street Hospital, has tripped and broken his leg. They're short-staffed there already so I'm to take over his work for a while.'

Lathom Street Hospital, she knew, was one of the three smaller peripheral hospitals that shared some of the facilities and staff with St Helen's. It was in the suburbs, about ten miles away.

'So you won't be seen here so much?' she asked.

'No. And to save travel, I'm going to live on the job. I'll take a couple of bags and sleep in the hospital.'

She couldn't help herself. 'You said you found it very easy to move on. Didn't want to surround yourself with—encumbrances.'

For a moment she thought she'd hurt him. He smiled wryly. 'A good doctor knows all the pressure points, where all the nerves are,' he said. 'I just wanted you to know why you won't be seeing so much of me.'

'To say goodbye.'

He shook his head again. 'Not goodbye, Delyth. I hope to come back soon. This is only *au revoir*.' He stood and walked out of the room.

What did he mean by that? she asked herself. Then she decided he'd meant nothing. They were just polite, parting phrases. When he came back he would still be her S.R. and she would learn a lot from him. They were colleagues, nothing more. She had to keep reminding herself of that.

She got up and made herself a cup of coffee at the tiny kitchen in the corner. Only when she had drunk half of it did she realise she had put three spoonfuls of powder in her cup. It tasted undrinkable, yet she'd finished half of it. Was she going mad? She threw the rest away, rinsed her cup and made herself more. Then she concentrated on her work.

Half an hour later the door opened again. This time it was Matt. She was pleased to see him—she needed some simple uncomplicated companionship. She had spent too much time with only her own thoughts.

'I've just dealt with a case of post-op hypotension,' he told her. 'Mrs Tennison had her appendicectomy this morning.'

'Serious?' she queried. A drop in blood pressure wasn't too unusual after general anaesthesia.

He shrugged. 'I don't think so. She seems well but a bit faint. Systolic blood pressure down just twenty millimetres. I've raised her legs and lowered her head, asked for her to be checked regularly.'

'Probably nothing,' she agreed.

The kettle was still warm and he made himself a coffee. 'Want another one?' he asked, pointing at her nearly empty cup. She didn't really, but she felt the need to share some thing with someone. And she liked Matt. He was simple, easy to be with. She nodded her assent.

'Heard about James going?' he asked her cautiously when they were sitting together at the table.

'Yes. He dropped in here a while ago.'

'We'll miss him. A bit frightening, but I think I've learned more from him than from Peter Kenny.'

'True,' she said, 'he's a good teacher.'

Matt sat silently, stirring his coffee far more than was necessary. 'You'll bore a hole in the bottom of your cup,' she pointed out.

He reddened a little, laid his spoon down and took a big mouthful of the hot liquid. Then he coughed and spluttered, and both of them laughed. 'Sorry,' he croaked, 'I was thinking of something else.'

'Going to tell me?'

The direct question seemed to throw him. He sipped more coffee, this time without spluttering. Then, with an obvious effort, he said, 'I thought you and James were getting quite…close.'

It was honest of him. But she wasn't going to be equally honest back. 'I like him a lot. But there's nothing…long term or serious between us.' Then, with more conviction than she really felt, she went on, 'In fact, there's nothing at all between us now.'

Matt was quick. '"Between us *now*"?' he questioned. 'You mean there was—?'

She wouldn't be cross-examined. 'I meant what I said,' she interrupted. 'Nothing between us apart from the fact that I like and admire him. Why d'you ask?'

'I want to take you out myself,' he blurted.

She looked at him in silence. He was tall, quite good-looking and for such a big man, appealing in a little-boy way. He was amiable, and she liked his company. But he wasn't James Owen.

And James Owen was nothing to her, she reminded herself.

'Look,' she said gently, 'we're both house officers, working ludicrous hours and taking what are, for us, big decisions. We've got no time for passion or heated relationships. We've just got to survive. I like you but I'm not ready for anything heavy.'

He persisted. 'So can I take you for a nice light-hearted drink tonight? Just you and me?'

'Do you *mean* light-hearted?' she questioned dubiously.

'Cross my heart, I do.'

'Then I'd love to go out with you.' When she saw the sheer delight on his face she felt a pang of guilt. I *have* warned him, she thought. What more can I do? And the idea of a simple uncomplicated evening was attractive.

She phoned Megan that night, just to chat and ask after Charles. After the usual exchanges Megan asked, 'And how're you and James?'

She should have known Megan would ask and wouldn't be put off. But Delyth intended to try. 'You sound like my big sister,' she said.

'I am your big sister and I take my big sisterly duties very seriously. You're avoiding the question so I already know the answer. What went wrong?'

She might as well be honest. She knew Megan would probe until she got the truth. 'We had a wonderful day. I thought we were getting on really well. Then he told me he just didn't want a...real relationship. He's not willing to give himself, wants to travel light.'

'Did he say why?'

Delyth thought she knew, but wasn't going to give Megan full details. 'He's had a...troubled life, Megan. He doesn't want more pain.'

'That shows in his face. How d'you feel, little sister?'

'I'll get over it.'

Thoughtfully Megan said, 'Delyth, perhaps he wasn't for ou right now. But I want you to know that I like him and nink an awful lot of him. What are you going to do now?'

'Go out with another hospital doctor,' Delyth said spir-edly.

Megan gulped with laughter. 'That's the idea. Fight back. Keep in touch and remember there're always other men.'

Delyth replaced the receiver. Did she want to fight back? Did she want another man?

In fact, it was four days before she could go out with Matt. She didn't see anything more of James—instead, she saw eter Kenny and even Mr Forrester. Both took a ward round. oth were quite good, but they were slower and didn't have he same flair as James. Neither took her and Matt into the orridor and gave them a carefully worked-out list of things o think about. But she pressed on.

She saw quite a lot of Matt, of course, and noted with ad pleasure that he was more careful of her, more consid-rate now she had agreed to go out with him. When invited to her room he was more ready to leave when asked. When he asked her about going out he didn't do it in front f their other friends. She saw he didn't want to go out in group. He wanted her to himself.

Both were now certain they could get out on Tuesday ight. On Monday night he said, 'There's this place called alanquin. I thought we might have dinner there.'

She looked at him doubtfully. 'I read about it in the paper. Minor royalty and people out of *Vogue*.'

He was pleased she knew of it. 'Yes, that's the place. It hould be good.'

She knew she'd have to choose her words carefully. Matt, I don't want you dressed up in your best suit and me a long dress. I'd much rather have a quieter meal some-

where near and be back earlier. We've got to work o
Thursday, you know, and we could be called in. Why n
keep the posh place until we've got something to celebrate'

He looked at her stonily. 'I can afford it, you know.'

'I know you can. But I'm not looking forward to goin
out to eat. I'm looking forward to going out with you.
couldn't relax at the Palanquin.'

It was the right thing to say, and his face relaxed. 'OI
we'll go somewhere closer.'

In the end one of the older doctors recommended him
an Italian restaurant in Covent Garden. Delyth had heard
it but had never been. They took a taxi there, had Parn
ham, spaghetti with a seafood sauce and ice cream. Th
house wine was just fine. Then they walked along th
Embankment, something she really liked. 'I love the lights
she told him. 'They remind me of Llandudno and the Riv
Conway.'

He laughed. 'You should see it where I live. Flat an
desolate and dreary.'

'It's still the Thames. It's history.'

As they strolled along he took her hand. She let him. H
had been good company all night—she suspected he wa
deliberately suppressing the brasher side of his nature. H
wanted to make an impression on her, wanted her to lik
him. The sad thought crept in that she would have bee
really happy if it hadn't been for her memories of Jame
Then she pushed the thought down.

When they got back to the residence they made tea an
drank it in her room. When they had finished it he kisse
her goodnight, not too passionately, and told her he wasn
going to try to stay. She told him she thought he was nic

Over the next fortnight they went out quite regularl
They went to the jazz night again. Often they had to go o
with Matt's group of friends, who seemed to expect i
Delyth was quite happy with this, Matt less so. 'Always wit

the gang,' he grumbled gently. 'I never seem to have you to myself.'

'Your fault for being so popular,' she reproved him. 'You've got lots of friends and I thought you liked going out in a group.'

He gave her a rueful smile. 'I'd rather be just with you.'

She was taking the bloods one morning when the junior nurse called her to the phone. 'It's Dr Owen for you,' she said. Delyth was glad of the warning. It gave her a chance to prepare herself. She was shocked at how her heart lurched at just the sound of his name. She was supposed to be getting over him!

Hearing his voice, it was worse. She hadn't heard from him for nearly three weeks, but the pain came back in its entirety.

'Hello, Delyth, it's James. Work going OK? Are you coping with everything?' His voice was cautious.

'Plenty of work but I'm coping with it,' she said shakily.

'Coping with the work,' he muttered. 'Good.' Then he seemed to get a grip on what he was thinking and his voice became firmer. 'Delyth, I want a favour. If you can't do it, or don't want to, then please say so. I should be most upset if you did something that you might find…awkward.'

'I'll refuse if I want to,' she assured him. 'What do you want?'

'Peter Kenny suggested you and checked your roster. I phoned him first. You should be able to fit it in.'

She felt a vague sense of annoyance that James hadn't asked her directly for his favour, then put the feeling behind her. 'I'll do what I can. So, tell me, what is it?'

He sounded almost embarrassed. 'It's silly really. You know I'm a runner when I get time? Well, the club I run with is putting on a half-marathon next Sunday, round one of the parks in North London. We've got quite a lot taking part. St John's Ambulance people will be helping us, but the doctor we had on site has let us down. Can you do it?'

It was an unusual request. 'I don't know much about sports injuries,' she told him. 'What will I be expected to do?'

'Probably not a lot. The committee just felt they wanted a doctor handy, and our insurance company asks for it. If you don't do it then I shall have to. So I'm asking you to spoil your Sunday afternoon so I can enjoy mine.'

'I'd like to do it,' she told him, 'and it won't spoil my afternoon. But just remember that I've never dealt with sports injuries or exhaustion before.'

He seemed relieved. 'You'll be working with people who know more about it than you do, and you'll probably enjoy learning something. But we need a doctor as a last line of defence—heart attack or something like that. There'll be a mini-treatment room set up by the sports pavilion. You don't need to organise or bring anything except a white coat.'

'I'll be there. Give me the address.'

He didn't ring off after giving her the details she needed. Instead, there was a pause. 'I'm…glad I feel that I can ask a favour of you,' he said eventually, 'and I'm glad that you're willing to do it.'

'You should know that I'd do a lot more for you than this,' she said bitterly, and rang off. She was suffering. Let him suffer too.

Mid-morning on Sunday she took a train to a distant London suburb. James had left her a message offering to pick her up. She had left him a reply saying it wasn't necessary. She quite enjoyed her long trip, trundling through new bits of the city.

She was always surprised at the amount of parkland there was in London. As she walked from the station to the park

he knew she was on the right road as there were young
men and women in tracksuits trotting past her. Eventually
he found the park and was directed to the sports pavilion.

There was a marquee to one side of the pavilion. She
entered to be greeted by the evocative scent of cut grass,
canvas and embrocation. And there was James coming towards her, dressed in an old blue tracksuit, the jacket open
to show the thin singlet underneath.

She wasn't prepared for the sudden rush of longing she
felt. She'd thought she had her feelings well under control—
now she discovered she didn't. She loved him! Even if he
didn't love her.

He was looking at her cautiously. Perhaps something of
what she felt showed in her face. She forced herself to smile
at him.

'I'm glad you could come, Delyth,' he said. 'It's purely
selfish. If you're here I can take part in the run.'

'A man must have his exercise,' she told him, and he had
the grace to look uncomfortable.

'Afterwards I could drive you back to the hospital,' he
said. 'Perhaps on the way we might—'

'There's no need, I've got a return ticket. But you can
show me what my duties are here.'

He looked at her stone-face, then apparently realised that
it was going to be strictly business between them. 'Of
course. All the first aid is run by John Williams here. You'll
find him very experienced, very friendly.'

John Williams turned out to be a bright-eyed, bearded
man in his late fifties, an obvious enthusiast. He introduced
her to his team. They didn't seem to resent Delyth at all,
but when James had gone she felt she had to make some
excuse.

'I doubt I'll be able to do anything as well as you,' she
said. 'I've only been a doctor for a few weeks so give me

any job you want. I have worked as a nurse. I'm very happy
to bandage sprains and see to cuts.'

He beamed at her. 'That's a very generous offer. I always
wanted to be a doctor myself, but I had to leave school to
go into insurance and this has been my hobby for the past
forty years. We don't usually need a doctor, but when we
do we need one badly. We'll be glad of your help.'

He glanced at his watch. 'There's little to do here now.
Why don't you go and watch the race start? It'll be in ten
minutes.'

Once outside she realised it was a well-organised event.
About five hundred were taking part, and were carefully
martialled in stages. The first stretch of the race was across
the park where there was plenty of open ground. The runners would space themselves, before making a second cir-
cuit and out onto the road. There was the countdown on the
PA system, then the great line of runners moved forward.
At first they seemed just a solid mass, but soon they broke
up as the faster runners streaked ahead.

She didn't see James. But she waited for ten minutes until
the leaders had reached the top of the park and come running back. Then she saw him. He wasn't with the first group
but was lying about twenty-fifth. She didn't want him to see
her, and so she stood in the shade of a tree. He was dressed
in blue shorts and a white singlet. Now she realised why he
walked so fast. His legs were long and he seemed to stride
effortlessly. And on his face was a curious expression, half
contentment, half determination. Delyth went back to the
tent.

'There'll be a few with exhaustion,' John told her.
'There're always one or two who haven't quite trained hard
enough but think it doesn't matter. Fortunately it's not too
hot, otherwise we'd have some with heat prostration—that
can get quite nasty. Had to send one or two to hospital in
the past. Blisters, of course, cuts and scratches when people

fall over, occasional sprains. But there'll be nothing for an hour or so so we'll all have a coffee.'

There was a rustling at the marquee door behind them, the sobbing of a child. 'Please, is there a doctor here?' an anguished voice called.

Delyth thought it polite to let John look at the case first. He moved over to where a young mother was clutching a wailing child, and led them both gently to a bed. Delyth followed him. When she saw the blood on the child's sleeve she didn't need John's beckoning arm to tell her that she was needed.

'He was playing on the wall by the trees,' the woman sobbed, 'and he fell off against this fence. There was a big nail sticking out and it dragged right down his arm.'

John was efficiently cutting off the little boy's shirt sleeve, a pad held against the still bleeding wound. Delyth pulled on a pair of rubber gloves. 'What's your little boy's name?' she asked gently. 'Are you his mother?'

'Yes, I'm Debbie Wright and this is Wayne. He's just seven. Is he going to be all right? Look at all the blood!'

John looked at Delyth, then waved over one of his assistants. 'Go and sit down a minute, Debbie, and we'll get you a hot drink. When you feel better come and hold Wayne's hand.' Debbie was led away, and John and Delyth bent over the whimpering little boy.

It didn't take either of them long to make a decision. Carefully Delyth wiped away the blood from the long cut and eased out a couple of obvious pieces of rusty metal. She looked at John and shook her head. 'It's beyond me here and with this equipment. He'll have to go to A and E. I think there may be some deep tissue damage. We'll just put a pad on and phone for an ambulance.'

He smiled at her. 'I'm glad you said that. You're the doctor, but it looks to me like a job that's going to take a consultant. I'll keep him warm and talk to him. You go an tell his mother what's happening.'

Debbie wasn't as happy with the decision. The sweet te and biscuits had cheered her up considerably. 'You're a doc tor, aren't you?' she asked. 'Why can't you stitch him up'.

'I want someone more expert than me to look at that cut. Delyth said carefully. 'It might need specialist attention.'

'I knew something like this would happen when we cam to the park. That one's always in trouble. And I was goin to go out tonight.'

'Come and put your arm round him,' Delyth said. 'Th ambulance will soon be here.'

In fact, it was remarkably quick. Delyth wrote a quic note to the A and E staff and said goodbye to their nov silent little charge. Debbie climbed into the ambulance an said nothing.

John winked at Delyth. 'Don't expect thanks every time he said.

After that there were the first casualties from the race The organisers had arranged for there to be cars waitin around the route. They now brought in those who were i trouble. There was nothing too serious, as John had said– a few blisters and a man who had sprained his ankle slippin off the pavement.

Then there was a potentially more serious case. An olde man, George Norris, was brought in—she guessed he'd b in his late forties. He was showing obvious signs of distres complaining of dizziness and nausea. 'I was doing so well. he told her, 'up there with people half my age.'

'Very good,' she told him. 'Do you train regularly?'

It turned out that he hadn't been running as often as h used to. 'But I'm still as good as I always was. Plenty c running in me still. I was doing fine, then suddenly— couldn't go on any more.'

'Just lie still, Mr Norris,' she told him. 'There's a couple
things we want to check.'

Both pulse and breathing were rapid, even though he'd
opped running twenty minutes before. His face was pale
d clammy. One of the men who had brought him in said
at George had been sitting by the roadside and that when
'd tried to stand he'd temporarily lost consciousness.
ncope, she thought—not enough blood pressure.

'Did you have much to drink as you ran, Mr Norris?'

'Don't hold with it. I always lose weight when I run.
od for you.'

'In your case, I'm not so sure.' She told him to drink
hat he could and rest on the cot provided. She would check
him again in a few minutes. 'Quite frankly, I think
u've overdone it,' she told him. 'You're exhausted.
efore you do any more running you're to see your GP and
t a thorough check-up.'

'I've never felt as bad as this before. I will.'

There was another lull. 'The first runners are in sight,'
hn told her. 'D'you want to go and watch the finish? It's
ly a few yards from here. If we need you we'll send for
u.'

She was tempted, and gave in. 'I'd like to watch,' she
id, 'but, please, do send for me if there's anything I can
.' She took off her white coat and walked over to where
e finishers would be channelled into lines.

The first man sprinted up to the line. He was small, thin,
rdly an ounce of fat on him. He held up his arm to ac-
owledge the cheers of the spectators. After him there was
bunch of a twenty or so, and then she saw James. Her
art beat faster. She had to admit to herself that she hadn't
me out to watch the end of the race. She'd come to see
mes.

His singlet and shorts were soaked with sweat, his hair
eaked with it. He was in a group of four men. As they

neared the finishing line three of them tried to sprint a
pulled away from James. She saw the rictus of strain on l
face as he forced unwilling muscles to pump faster. l
chest heaving, he caught up with them. The crowd saw t
little personal competition and began to shout. All four r
faster. But somehow James managed to creep ahead a
hold his tiny lead until he ran first into the finishing alle
She saw him collect his place card, trot slowly for anotl
few yards, finally stop and bow his head to his knees.

She walked over to him. 'Congratulations,' she said. 'Y
nearly killed yourself in the last few yards to come thir
first instead of thirty-fourth.' Then she smiled to show s
didn't mean it.

'Trust a woman to hit a man when he's down,' he gaspe
'How has your afternoon been?'

'I've enjoyed it and learned a few things. But we've be
largely trouble-free.' She paused a minute. 'What are y
doing?'

He was bent over, his leg straight, the toe pointing u
wards. 'Stretching the muscles and tendons,' he told her.
you do this after every race you won't get stiff.' He chang
position to stretch the other leg.

'I must remember that.' She could smell, feel, the ma
ness of him. Curiously she asked, 'You enjoyed pushi
yourself to the limit, didn't you?'

'If you don't push yourself, it's not worth doing. Dely
thanks again for giving me the chance of running.'

'I'd better get back to the tent,' she said.

The tent was filling up. John told her that some of t
runners just came in to lie down. They didn't exactly fe
ill but they wanted to rest in comfort. She looked at one
two minor problems, checked a couple of people w
looked slightly more ill. And she found George Norris, s
ting up on his cot, eagerly talking to another runner.

'I feel much better, Doctor,' he told her eagerly. 'I thi

know where I went wrong. It won't happen the next time
—'

'Look,' she told him, 'you have to see your GP. What
appened to you can be serious. Next time it might not be
simple drink and a rest.' She took his pulse. 'Now, lie
own for another half-hour.'

'I know what my GP will say. Stop running. Take up
omething stupid like golf instead.'

'If your heart goes into fibrillation—starts beating irreg-
arly—you could dislodge a small blood clot. If it reaches
e brain the consequences of that are far worse than a rest
 a medical tent. We're talking about a stroke, possible
aralysis. All I'm saying is talk to your GP. Otherwise you
ight be sorry.'

'Will he do as he's told?' she asked John a few minutes
ter.

John looked thoughtful. 'Possibly,' he said, 'though a lot
f these men are fanatics.'

'You're telling me. I've met some.'

It was unfortunate that James should pick that moment to
alk up behind them. He had heard what she'd said but he
oked at her expressionlessly. He was in his old blue track-
it again and she noticed that he'd washed his face and
air.

'I can take over from you now, Delyth,' he said, 'unless
ou want to stay a bit longer with me?'

She shook her head. 'I think I'll go back to the hospital.
hank you for the chance to work with the group. I've found
 very interesting and I think I've learned something. But
ere's nothing else for me here.'

He knew what she meant. As she turned to go she saw
e anger in his eyes again. But he'd had his chance. She
st wasn't interested in a casual relationship.

'Once again, thank you for all you've done,' he said
arshly.

'It was nothing.' She turned to John Williams, her voi
consciously more pleasant. 'I've enjoyed being here, Joh
Hope to see you again some time.'

'You'll always be welcome,' he assured her.

She was aware of the two men looking at her back as s
walked across the park, and wondered miserably if th
were talking about her. This had not been a good idea. S
had thought she would be professional with James, one co
league helping another. Instead, all her previous pains h
resurfaced. Did he have *no* feelings for her? Didn't he kn
what he had just made her suffer? He was harder, dark
than she had thought.

CHAPTER SIX

'WHERE have you been? I've been looking for you.'

It was too bad that the first person Delyth had to meet when she entered the residence was Matt. He'd had a morning shift. It was now about half past five, and she hadn't enjoyed the trip back half as much as she'd enjoyed the trip out. She rather resented his question, but knew this was nothing to do with him. She was the ill-tempered one.

For a moment she considered hiding the truth, then decided not to. It had been her decision to go. 'I've been doctor in charge at a half-marathon in north London,' she told him.

He looked away. He knew about James's hobby. 'You've been out with James Owen,' he accused her.

She wondered why she had to justify herself to him, but she knew he meant well. 'I haven't been out with him. I did him a favour,' she said soothingly. 'In fact, I enjoyed myself and I came straight back.'

'Not going out with him?'

'Why should I? Anyway, he didn't ask me.' It wasn't quite a lie.

Matt appeared to be placated by this. 'So you're still coming to the jazz with us tonight?'

'I'm looking forward to it,' she told him honestly.

She did enjoy the jazz at the Old City Walls that night. She was with a group of friends and they had a happy, noisy time. Back at the residence there was a bustling party, shouting and singing, drinking tea and making cheese on toast. But they all had to work the next day and it soon ended.

She found herself in her bedroom with Matt. When sh
sat on her bed he came to sit beside her and kissed he
gently at first. She was happy with this and kissed him bac
But his kisses became more passionate, more demandin
She felt his hand stray down her front and cautiously strok
her breast. She didn't really object, but…she had to be fai
Gently, she pushed away his hand and took his arms fro
round her.

'You can kiss me in my bedroom, Matt, and I quite lik
it,' she said. 'But I'll tell you now I don't want to go an
further. We've both got enough to think about now witho
that. I like you, I'm sorry, but that's how it is.'

He smiled sheepishly, then kissed her again, a soft, almo
brotherly kiss. 'That's fine by me,' he said. 'I like you a lo
Delyth. I think you're worth waiting for. We'll get to kno
each other more and see what happens.'

It was a generously spirited remark and she liked hi
more for it. Quickly kissing him on the cheek, she sai
'What happens now is that we both get some sleep. Go
bed. I'll give you a shout in the morning.' Smiling, he lef

She was tired now—she was always tired—but sh
couldn't sleep. As she lay in bed she thought about her li
and the two men in it. Or the one man in it?

'I'm a typical Essex man,' Matt had said. But he wasn
Now he was turning from a brash young person into som
one who was hard-working and attractive. There was se
sitivity there, she thought, and a genuine caring for he
Would she come to love him?

This she didn't know. She thought she might, but as y
there had been no blinding flash, no absolute conviction th
this was the man for her. The odd power that she sometim
had was not there to be tapped or referred to—it struck whe
it wished. And it had been so wrong about James. She ju
didn't know if Matt could be the man for her.

What about James? She realised now how little she ha

ught about him since that wonderful afternoon and that
palling evening. It was as if her mind had blanked him
as being too painful to consider.

The two men's faces flashed before her. Matt, handsome,
en and friendly. James as he had been earlier today,
eat-streaked, grim and determined, even in some pain.
ere was a darkness about James that wasn't present in
att. The sad conviction grew that James was still part of
life. She didn't know how, but somehow he was going
affect her. She shivered. It might be for the bad.

week later she was sitting in the doctors' room on the
rd, wrestling again with her paperwork. This time it was
et of TTOs—To Take Out forms. Often these were dealt
h by someone senior, but she'd been asked to handle a
v. They were the forms that patients took with them when
y were discharged, and which entitled the patients to
gs from the hospital pharmacy. As ever, there was an
ful lot of copying to be done.

James walked in. She was shocked. She hadn't seen him
ce the race, and before that hadn't seen him for three
eks, but after all this time her body still reacted to his
seness. Her heart beat faster and she knew her face col-
ed slightly. She missed him! By this time surely she was
itled to a little peace? She *had* to get over him.

He looked tired. In the past she had thought him imper-
us to the strains all the rest of them felt, but now there
re lines by his eyes, a deepening in the creases by his
uth. He still looks gorgeous, an impertinent part of her
nd suggested, and she struggled to push the thought away.

'You look as if you've been having a hard time,' she said.
e hadn't intended to be so personal, so concerned, when
y first met again, but the words just slipped out.

'They've been working me hard at Lathom Street. There
s a bit of a backlog of operations. I tried to get it down.

Mostly just run-of-the-mill stuff—varicose veins and so
Still, they cause enough misery. Did a gastrectomy yest
day—some poor devil with a bleeding ulcer in his stoma
Anyway, they've got a replacement now so I've got a cou
of days off then I'm back here. How have you been?'

'Busy. Just the usual, but I think I'm learning. I'm
joying the work.'

'It's good to concentrate,' he agreed.

'It certainly takes your mind off other things,' she s
acidly, then cursed herself silently. He'd tried to offer he
reasonable, boring conversation about work, something th
could build a professional relationship on. And sh
wrecked it. She looked up, rather shame-faced, and fou
him grinning at her.

'All good doctors have a reservoir of toughness,' he sa
'They have to be able to defend themselves. *You* take
fight into the enemy camp.'

Now she *was* embarrassed. She was desperately trying
think of some flippant remark when the phone rang.
picked it up, listened, offered it to her. 'For you.'

'Dr Price here,' she barked, grateful for any respite.
first she didn't recognise the voice on the other end of
line. It was low, possibly drugged, and there was the ca
of pain in it. 'Megan!' she gasped. 'Are you all right?'

'I've been better,' her sister said. 'I'm just realising t
there might be something good about having a doctor in
family.'

'What happened? Are you ill?'

There was the sound of Megan trying to laugh. 'Not
injured. I'm trying to persuade myself that it's a joke. I f
off a stool in the kitchen, Delyth. And I was standing
tiptoe. Anyway, I sprained my ankle. Not just an ordin
sprain, but a tendon-tearing good job. I was in agony, a
the A and E officer I saw said it was worse than if
broken it.'

'How did you get to hospital?' Delyth broke in. She knew what absolute pain a sprained ankle could cause.

'I lay on the floor and phoned for Charles next door. He let himself in and called an ambulance. Anyway, the thing is, I'm largely immobilised and since I can't work I thought I'd have a bit of home comfort. I'm going back to Mum's cooking. But I don't fancy the train journey, and I certainly can't drive, so I wondered if you could drive me there on your next free day.'

'Of course I'll drive you,' Delyth said at once, 'and, in fact, I'm off tomorrow.'

'Super! You haven't got a car. We'll take my old Land Rover.'

'The Land Rover? Fine,' Delyth said doubtfully. The thing was, she wasn't a very confident driver. She'd passed her test, of course, but after that she hadn't had much practice. And Megan's heavy vehicle wasn't the Mini she'd learned in. Still, she'd cope. 'I want to get an early start. I'll be round at yours about half past six in the morning,' she told her sister, and replaced the receiver.

'I'll drive you both,' a voice said.

She turned to look at James. 'Why should you?' she asked.

'Because I've got the day off and nothing much to do. Because I very much fancy a trip into Wales. Because I drove a Land Rover all the time in Africa. Because I could tell by your face that you weren't really looking forward to driving, and I need my junior staff to stay happy.'

They were all good reasons and not one of them was the one she wished to hear. For a moment she thought about asking Matt, but she knew he was on duty. And being driven by someone was preferable to driving herself so... 'That's very kind of you,' she said. 'I'll accept.'

Megan had borrowed crutches from the hospital and could hobble a few feet, but James picked her up effortlessly and

carried her downstairs. He established her in a nest of blankets and pillows on the back seat of her tatty old diesel Land
Rover. Then he went to fetch her cases.

Megan hadn't apparently been surprised when James had
turned up with Delyth. 'Has your affair restarted, then?' she
asked while James was upstairs. 'Not that I'm objecting. I
like him and I'm glad of his help.'

'We haven't restarted anything. He just wanted a trip into
Wales.'

'Of course he did. D'you think Mum will like him? You
have warned her, haven't you?'

'I phoned to say a colleague had offered to drive us,'
Delyth said stiffly.

'I'll bet she gets the best china out.'

Then James returned, Delyth strapped herself into the
front seat and they were off.

She might have guessed that James was a good driver.
He drove as he operated, quickly and decisively, threading
his way through the morning London traffic. She thought it
typical of him that he had checked the road map and me-
morised the route out of the city. She would have got there
eventually, but it seemed no time before they were on the
slip road to the M1, driving north.

'I love driving Land Rovers,' he told them. 'I had one of
my own in Africa. When I had an hour to spare—which
was practically never—I used to drive out into the bush. No
roads, for once no patients—just me, the bush and solitude.'

'And insects,' Megan put in from the back.

He laughed. 'Oh, yes, indeed, the insects. Who could forget them?'

He accelerated when they were on the motorway. The
diesel engine was noisy and it wasn't too easy to talk.
Megan was still in some pain. Delyth had given her a couple

powerful analgesics, and she quickly dozed off. 'I could
ke over for a bit, if you like,' she shouted to James.

'I'm enjoying myself, don't worry. Why don't you doze
o? Your seat will recline.'

She had one quick glance at his profile. He was absorbed
his driving, half smiling, his eyes calculating what was
ppening ahead. So he didn't want to talk to—shout at—
r. Very well. It was his decision. After all, she was tired
d it had been an early start. She would get some sleep.
ie pulled at the lever that caused her seat to fall back.

e must have been more tired than she'd realised. The next
ing she remembered was being gently shaken. 'I can see
e hills of Wales in the distance,' he said. 'Want to wake
d have a look?'

She struggled awake. 'Where are we?'

'Just come off the M54. We're on the A5 now. Soon be
Shrewsbury.'

'That far! We're past Birmingham. I've been asleep for
ours!'

'Sleep while you can. I do. Are you glad to be going
ome?'

They were less than an hour from her village. She felt a
rtain excitement, but... 'I'm partly glad,' she said. 'I've
ent most of my life in rural Wales and I love it. But
ondon's been good for me. Perhaps I was getting a bit
arochial—a bit narrow.'

'What will you do when you finish your house jobs,
elyth? What's your future career to be?'

This was a good question. After pondering, she said, 'Un-
 recently all I wanted was to be a Welsh GP. I worked a
t with our local one, Alun Roberts. He helped me and I
pposed I wanted to be like him. But now...well, I am
njoying hospital work.' She paused for a moment and then
id, 'There aren't many female surgeons, are there?'

'Not many,' he agreed, 'but some, and those I ha
worked with have been very good. Now, where do we
from here?'

The hills were closer now, and at her direction they turn
off the main highway. Then they were in a maze of ti
roads, known to her since she was a child, threading th
way round hills and past farms. Behind them Megan sat u
wakened by the swaying as they negotiated more and mc
tight bends. Then they were in the village where she
grown up. There was the post office, the bakery, the ti
primary school, the single pub. It was an odd sensation.
wasn't the same as when she'd been away at universi
Then she'd known she'd be coming back. Now…perha
she had left for good.

Finally they turned into the drive of the house. Behind
she could see the long gleaming lines of her father's gree
houses. Her mother came to the door, warned by the crun
of the tyres on the gravel. Then it hit her. It was *good*
be home!

Her father was away, giving a paper at a conference
market gardening and its place in the rural economy. 'I
was dreading it,' her mother said cheerfully, 'but he phon
last night and said some of the people there actually kn
what they were talking about. There's talk of part of a te
vision programme being shot down here.'

'The village will like that,' said Megan, now lying on t
couch.

'Will Grandad be on the telly?' asked Robert, one
Delyth's numerous nephews and nieces. Her sister Luc
was a music teacher who had married a local farmer, a
she'd brought her three children over for the day.

'He might,' said Lucie. 'Why?'

'I help Grandad dig sometimes,' said four-year-c
Robert. 'And weed and carry things. Will I be on telly, to

'You can sit on the draining board and help me with the peas,' Delyth's mother said, picking up her grandson. 'And don't eat so many this time.'

Lucie winked at Delyth and James. 'He spends more time here in the garden than he does watching television,' she said. 'Strange child. Sometimes I worry about him. Now, Delyth, never mind the medicine—are you getting any singing done?'

James had been introduced and quietly accepted. He sat in the giant rocking chair, watching Delyth and her family. After an hour they all went to the giant conservatory for lunch. It was still warm enough to eat out there.

'We call it a conservatory,' Delyth told James as they arranged themselves round the trestle table, 'but, as you can see, really it's just another of my father's greenhouses.' She waved at the neatly arrayed growing plants.

'My husband's a lucky man, Dr Owen,' her mother told James. 'His job is his hobby.'

'I think he's lucky in more ways that that,' James said, 'and will you call me James?'

It was a good lunch—fresh salad from the greenhouses, their own eggs, bread baked that morning and ham from the local butcher. Delyth had almost forgotten what really fresh food was like. The hospital canteen did very well, she supposed, but it was nothing like home cooking.

After the meal Mrs Owen turned to James and said, 'You've driven all the way here and I gather you're going to do all the driving back. If I know my two daughters, they slept most of the journey. Would you like to go into the study with your tea and catnap for an hour? You'll find it refreshing and I'll see you're not disturbed.'

He smiled at her. 'You should have been a surgeon's wife. That's a great idea.'

So James slept while Delyth, her mother, Lucie and her two children wandered round the greenhouses. There was a lot of family gossip to catch up on, a lot to tell about her new job. And it was good to feel the damp heat of the greenhouses, to smell and inspect the growing plants.

'He seems a nice man, this James,' her mother said. 'You say you're working for him?'

'He's the specialist registrar on my firm,' Delyth answered cautiously. 'He does a lot of the teaching.'

'Tell him if he ever wants a few days' break he can come and stay a while,' her mother said. 'I'd like to see him again.'

And that was all. Delyth smiled to herself. She should have known that she wouldn't be questioned on anything. Her mother knew instinctively what needed saying, what could be left unsaid. Her mother liked him.

When they returned to the house Lucie ordered Delyth to the main living room. 'It's the other end of the house from the study,' she said, 'and we won't disturb the sleeping doctor. I haven't heard you sing for six months. It's wicked!'

Megan hauled herself onto her crutches. 'I'm coming too,' she announced. 'I might even join in.'

Delyth blinked. But this had always been a house full of singing voices, and she realised it was another thing she had missed.

The house walls were solid, and they were some way from the study. James would sleep on. Lucie seated herself at the piano and played a couple of chords. 'Right,' she said, 'you know this.'

'This' was 'Bye-bye, Blackbird'. They had all sung it as children together, and she loved it. After it was finished they all sang 'In the Good Old Summertime' and then, more difficult, she sang 'September Song' alone.

It was now nearly the end of September.

'''When the autumn weather turns the leaves to flame, one hasn't got time for the waiting game''',' Delyth sang.

Her eyes closed as she moved towards the end. It always seemed to her one of the finest, saddest songs she knew.

There was silence as she finished. And then someone clapped. She opened her eyes to see James in the doorway. How long had he been there? Why hadn't she heard him arrive?

'That was truly lovely,' he told her gravely. 'But your mother sent me to tell you it's time we were moving.'

It made sense, of course. It was a long journey back and he had to be at work next morning. They had a farewell coffee, her mother stuffed a vast bag of sandwiches in the car, kisses all round and they were away.

'How d'you feel?' he asked her as they finally drove out of the well-loved village. 'Sorry to be leaving?'

She considered the question. 'Half-sorry. I grew up there. I have so many good memories, of family and friends. But I've started on a new path now. I'm learning to be a doctor. I'm looking forward to being at work tomorrow morning.'

She didn't tell him she was slightly apprehensive about the next few hours. How would she manage in his company?

'It was very good of you to drive us,' she said. 'I suppose I could have managed, but you made it all seem so much easier.'

'I'm enjoying it. And it was a very pleasant break.' He pulled out to slide expertly around a lorry. 'And I did enjoy meeting your family. I can see the attraction of having so many people caring for you.'

'But you still don't want one of your own?' It slipped out before she had a chance to stop herself. Why did she have to ask something so stupid?

'I can manage,' he replied bleakly. 'I've made my decision and I'll stick to it.'

She could think of no answer to that.

CHAPTER SEVEN

DELYTH knew Mary Cooney was going to be a squeamis patient. Mary was young, tried to act tough, but there ha been fear in her eyes as she'd looked at the IV lines drippin into the arms of other patients. 'You're going to cut a hol in my arm? Put one of those things inside it?'

'We have to put drugs straight into your bloodstream. Delyth explained. 'It's a bit uncomfortable but it doesn' really hurt.' She could tell by the rigidity of her patient' body that Mary didn't believe her so she smeared EMLA anaesthetic cream over the selected veins and left a dressin over it for half an hour. Now there should be no feeling a all.

Mary was right-handed so Delyth picked a vein in the lef arm in the cubital fossa, the hollow just in front of the elbov joint. She tightened the tourniquet about the arm. 'Don' look if you don't want,' she suggested to Mary. Mar squeezed her eyes shut.

Delyth eased the needle through the skin and subcutane ous fat, then felt the resistance give way as she pierced th vein. A drop or two of blood appeared in the base of th cannula, the tube that would be inserted into the vein. The it was simply a matter of gently withdrawing the metal style which had done the actual cutting and advancing the plasti cannula further into the vein. It was done. She secured th cannula to the arm with a dressing, and took off the tour niquet. 'All done,' she told Mary. 'We can give you a dri now.'

'Nothing to it,' Mary said.

Matt was in the doctors' room. 'Good day yesterday?' he asked pleasantly.

'I went back home for the day. My sister hurt her ankle and James Owen drove us both to my parents'.'

She could tell by the stillness of his shoulders that this wasn't the best news he'd ever heard. 'I thought you and James had fallen out,' he said. He managed to keep his voice neutral, but she knew what he was thinking.

'We get on together—we have to. I would have asked you to drive, but I knew you couldn't take the time off. So I was pleased when James offered to help.'

'And where does that leave me?' He was still trying to control his anger—she appreciated that.

She walked round the table to kiss him on the cheek. 'It leaves you as a hard-working house officer and a good friend of mine,' she said. 'Now, have you looked at those radiography referral forms?'

There was never time for long soul-searching sessions during the day. They were too busy. But just for a moment she wondered why she had to explain her actions to Matt. Then she found herself wondering if, had things been different, she would have wanted to explain things to James. There was no answer so she got on with her work.

Mid-morning, a call came up from A and E. 'Got you another client, an awkward one, Delyth. Doesn't speak a word of English. Apparently the police were called to a fight of some sort, and when they got there only this man was left. His pals deserted him. Police sent for an ambulance and have left us to sort things out. We don't know who he is, there's nothing at all in his pockets and we don't even know what language he speaks.'

Delyth grimaced. So much of her time was taken up with paperwork. The prospect of dealing with someone who couldn't offer a single fact filled her with horror. This could take for ever. 'Why are you we admitting him?' she asked.

'The usual contusions and bruises, but I doubt they're too important. He's had some kind of heavy blow to the head. We need to observe him for a couple of days. We've given him a skull CT—there's nothing too serious showing on it.'

Delyth nodded to herself. Computerised tomography, a form of X-ray, would reveal a lot of possible damage. Perhaps this patient wouldn't be too troublesome. 'Send him up,' she said. 'I'll see about a bed.'

The new patient was brought up on a trolley, his clothes in a basket at the bottom, his notes to hand. Delyth had him taken into a side ward, swished the curtains round and looked at the form she had to fill in. For the moment much of it would have to remain blank.

'I'll call you John,' she said, smiling at the dark man below her. 'That is, unless you can tell me your name?'

John was now conscious, his large eyes flashing, obviously frightened. But he didn't respond to her invitation. With a young nurse in attendance, Delyth carried out a full examination, explaining to the nurse what she was doing. She got rather a kick out of being a teacher for once, rather than a student.

There were tribal scars on John's cheeks, but they meant nothing to Delyth. She found John to be a youngish man, thin but not emaciated. He had been badly knocked about in the fight and there were several injuries that were obviously painful, but which she didn't think life-threatening. Delyth paid particular attention to the bruising to the chest. 'It's important to ensure there are no fractures or visceral injuries,' she explained to the young nurse. 'They might lead to hypotension—low blood pressure—and that can compound any brain damage.' But in this case she was reasonably sure there was no great damage.

She took blood and had it sent down for the blood gases to be checked, then went to look for Peter Kenny. She knew he was on the ward somewhere. Head injuries should always be referred to someone senior, she had been told.

Peter Kenny looked at her notes, and the patient, and decided there was no need to send for a neurosurgeon. 'Keep him under observation,' he said. 'Any serious deterioration, let me know. But I don't feel his injuries are too serious. Pity he can't talk to us.'

'Who d'you think he is?' Delyth asked.

Peter shrugged. 'Probably an illegal immigrant. This isn't our problem. You mustn't get involved, Delyth. Concentrate on the medical aspect. We just don't have the resources for social investigations.'

'Can we separate the two?'

'No,' he said, 'we can't. But we have to.'

She knew Peter was right, his apparent hardness was just a self-protecting mechanism. She'd have to develop it herself in time. But at present it was difficult.

The hospital had come across the problem of non-English speakers before. At intervals through the day people came onto the ward to try to speak to John in their native languages. St Helen's was a cosmopolitan hospital, and there were people there from many nationalities. But John responded to none of them. Delyth watched as one man spoke in a curious hissing language, and was sure there was the flash of intelligence on John's face. But he didn't reply.

'I thought he understood me, miss,' the man said. He was a worker in the boiler room. 'But I couldn't get him to talk back.'

'Well, thanks for trying,' she said.

John's case was only one of several she had to deal with. She turned to something else.

Next morning she was in the operating theatre, assisting Mr Forrester. This was work she thoroughly enjoyed, though Forrester was not quite as ready as James to let her try the simpler techniques. He was performing an aortic aneurysm repair. The wall of the aorta, the main artery of the heart, had stretched and become weakened, and it was necessary to replace a section of it with a man-made tube. Delyth practised suturing under his careful attention. Once again she wondered about being a surgeon herself, but decided this was not a good time to mention it.

When she got back on the ward after the morning's work, her mysterious patient had gone.

'His uncle came for him,' Matt explained. 'He was very polite, insisted that John could sign himself out. Apparently he's going to be a student here. I wasn't very keen on letting him go, but the uncle knew all the ropes. There was no way I could keep him here. I couldn't section him.'

Delyth frowned. 'What sort of man was this uncle?'

Matt shrugged. 'Like I said, always polite but obviously used to getting his own way. Quite well dressed, but he had two full gold teeth in the front. You don't often see those now. Said he'd bring John back to Outpatients. I got him to sign, and put his address underneath.'

He showed her the form that had been signed. And as she looked at it something struck her with the force of a nightmare. John was going to die. Worse than that... What was it? Worse than that... The room spun around her. She had never had a feeling as bad as this before.

She felt Matt's arm round her shoulder, felt him guide her to a chair. 'Are you OK, Delyth? You look faint.' She heard the concern in his voice.

'Yes, I'm fine. I'm just a bit...worried about this man.' She had told James about the power she had, but had never thought of telling Matt. For a moment she wondered why. Anyway, she certainly wasn't going to start now.

'We just can't go into people's personal problems,' Matt

said, kindly enough, 'and certainly not if they don't invite us to.'

'We're supposed to treat the whole person!'

'It's just not always possible. Now, d'you want to go back to your room to rest? I can cope with what's left here.' She knew he was being considerate, but that wasn't what she wanted.

'I'm all right. A quick coffee and I'll be back on the ward.' She had work to do.

That evening she had intended to sit quietly in her room, perhaps do a bit of background reading. But at half past eight she found she couldn't rest. Throwing on a coat, she went and climbed in one of the taxis that waited outside the hospital gates. She gave the driver the address the gold-toothed man had given as John's home—she just couldn't forget it.

It wasn't a long journey. The address didn't exist. The street was there, but it had never held any houses. In fact, one side of the street was a blank wall, the other a tiny park. 'It just ain't here, miss,' the taxi driver said after they'd been up and down the street twice. He consulted his *A-Z*. 'And there's no other street by that name in London.' She asked him to take her back.

'We just can't get involved,' Matt said over a cup of tea in the residence. 'It may be fishy, but that man left of his own free will. I don't know how he was persuaded to leave, but he was. Who d'you want to tell?'

Who could she tell—and tell them what? She didn't know.

She rang A and E and got the address of where the man had been found. It was the other side of the hospital from where she'd just been. She looked it up in her own *A-Z*, and guessed it wasn't the best of areas.

Now she seemed to be working on some kind of autopilot,

as if she were driven by some force other than her own free will. She went down a floor and borrowed a district nurse's uniform from a friend. It looked well on her and she admired herself in it, thinking it was smarter than her own greens or white coat. It would be easy for her to take a couple of hours off tomorrow afternoon—what she had in mind she could do then.

Next morning she wondered again if she was doing right. Should she confide in someone? She knew Matt wasn't the right one. The only other person would be James. Speedily she gave up the idea. She had to get James out of her life.

It was easy to arrange. She left the ward at lunchtime, changed into the nurse's uniform and put a blue mac over it. She took another taxi. The driver was surprised at the street name she gave him. 'Not a very nice neighbourhood, miss,' he said.

It was amazing how quickly London could change. In five minutes she travelled from an area of expensive shops and prosperous businesses to this littered, graffitti-scarred wilderness. There were large blocks of flats, with the odd brave flowerpots on the balconies. Most of the buildings were crumbling Victorian tenements. The few people she saw didn't look at her. She felt like a stranger in her own country.

Too soon she was at her destination. 'Want me to wait for you?' the taxi driver asked. 'This place looks a bit of a dump.'

'I'll be all right. I may be here a while.' She paid him and the black cab disappeared.

It was a cul-de-sac she walked down, not a residential street but little more than an alley. There were rough warehouses, a locked-up garage, a piece of derelict land. She got to the street end. The place was completely deserted. Not a person to be seen.

She thought she would turn back, find her way to the

earest main road and pick up a taxi to take her back. As
ne did so the certainty hit her again, so strongly that she
ad to lean against the dirty brick wall for support. Someone
eeded her help. Someone was dying, near, very near her.
t had never been like this before. It wasn't one person—it
as more than one. People were dying!

There was a stout door set back in the nearest warehouse.
he climbed to it up three crumbling steps, then frowned,
ightly surprised. A new, expensive-looking deadlock was
t by the side of the old keyhole. She looked around. There
as barbed wire along the top of every wall, tiny windows
ith bars across the inside. She hammered on the door.
here was no answer, and after five minutes she hammered
;ain. She had a feeling of being watched, and she thought
ie saw a shadow flit across the darkness behind the nearest
indow. She hammered a third time. It was almost an anti-
imax when the door was opened.

'Yes?' a tall man asked politely. He was black, but that
asn't surprising. Most of the people in the neighbourhood
ere black.

Now she had someone to speak to, Delyth wasn't quite
ıre of what to say. She hadn't planned this far ahead. She
ammered, 'Er...two days ago there was a fight outside
ere. A man was injured. D'you know anything about it?'

'I'm afraid not, miss. We do get some violence down
ere. There is a very troublesome public house down the
ad.'

'So you can't help me? The man was signed out of my
ospital. We think he may be seriously ill.'

'This is only an import-export agency. We bring goods
from my own country. I know of no one who has been
.'

'I see.' Her shoulders sagged. 'Sorry to have troubled
u. It was my mistake.'

'Not at all.' Smiling, the man moved to close the door.

He had two gold front teeth. She remembered Matt's d
scription of the person who had signed John out.

Quickly, she said, 'I'll make my report and the poli
will probably be round later.' She was lying as she'd nev
lied before, but the man didn't know that.

'Police? I see no need for them. Do come inside. We c
discuss it.'

Too late she realised her mistake. 'No, I have to go. I.

He had detected her suspicions. When she turned
grabbed her, hauled her backwards into the doorway. S
tried to wrench herself out of his grasp and grab for t
door. But she was unbalanced. She just turned her he
sufficiently to see him, not at all polite now, grasping a gre
lump of wood. It swung at her head and she couldn't duc
There was an explosion of agonising pain and she fell, pu
ting out a hand to save herself. There was another flash
pain in her hand, and then a merciful semi-darkness. S
slumped to the floor.

A tiny part of her brain was never quite extinguished. S
knew she was on the floor. She felt herself being turn
onto her back, dragged away from the doorway by t
shoulders. The man was shouting, but she didn't understa
him. Then someone else came and picked up her legs, a
she was carried, down, down. She didn't know where. It g
cooler.

Then there was the creak of another door opening. S
was dropped carelessly on a cold floor. Behind her a do
slammed to. Her nostrils detected a smell, a medical sme
a smell of illness, but like nothing else she'd smelt befo
Then she lost consciousness completely.

She was unconscious for only a minute or so. She awo
to coldness, her head and wrist agonising. She didn't wa
to open her eyes, she wanted to sleep, but consciousne
was rushing back. She felt a twinge of nausea, and to
deep breaths to stop herself vomiting—and that made h

come awake even faster. Why did her head and hand hurt so much? Somehow she managed to sit upright.

There was a dim light in the room, and by it she could see her right hand. Ugh! An automatic expression of disgust struck her. Two of her fingers were sticking out backwards at a ludicrous angle. They were dislocated. Without thinking, she grasped the two and yanked at them. She felt them click back into place. They hurt—but the pain was endurable. Then she realised there was another pain further back along her arm. Delicately, she tried to move her wrist. The feeling of crepitus—a bony grating—was unmistakable. Her wrist was broken. And she had an evil headache.

She felt her head. A trickle of blood, a great lump. It hurt, and she suspected it was going to hurt more, but she didn't think she was concussed. If I can think about it, and decide that I'm not concussed, then I'm probably not concussed, she told herself. Then she realised that her careful analysis of the situation was just a way of avoiding being afraid. The full horror of her situation broke over her. She had been attacked, imprisoned—goodness knew what might happen to her next. Things like this just didn't happen to people like her!

Nobody knew where she was. Where was she? She wished she had someone with her. She shut her eyes again, her mind filled with the silent screamed message. James! I'm here! Come and get me.

Then she decided that was foolish. She had to look after herself.

She pulled herself slowly to her feet and looked round. She was in a large, dimly lit cellar. There were no windows. The walls were stone and the ceiling low, the door behind her locked.

She wasn't alone. There was a groaning, the sighing and wheezing of breathing. And that smell! It wasn't just unwashed humanity, though that was part of it. There was the smell of illness. At the far side of the room were six truckle beds. She walked over to see who was in them.

On the way she found an open door leading to a lavatory and filthy washbasin. Running water on her hands, she splashed it over her face. Then, a little more alert, she went to inspect the beds.

Six beds with six men in them. All had the same tribal scars on their faces that John had. She recognised the third man—it was John. The men who were awake looked at her uncomprehendingly. She felt their foreheads—they all had a fever. John hadn't had a fever yesterday. What had brought it on so fast?

One man seemed to be most ill of all. She eased down the sheet covering him, trying not to gag at the smell. There was a rough dressing over his armpit. She peered at the ulcerous patch underneath. Then she turned to the next man and looked under his blanket. Her suspicions were confirmed. He had a large growth on his groin. She'd never come across it before, but she'd seen pictures, read accounts. The growth was a called a bubo. These men were affected by bubonic plague. In the Middle Ages it had been called the Black Death. And it was intensely infectious.

She went to sit on the floor on the far side of the room and thought. Clear, logical thinking took away some of the terror of her situation. Half-remembered notes came back to her, things she'd thought she'd never have to deal with. The last outbreak in England had been in the 1920s, she thought and occasional cases since in people coming from abroad. It could be very infectious, if it was airborne, usually carried from human to human by sneezing. Atishoo, Atishoo, all fall down. That was the nursery rhyme, and it referred to the plague. But she hadn't heard anyone sneezing. That was good. Presumably these men had the flea-borne disease, and that was far less infectious.

There was good news. Treatment was easy. Tetracycline

doxycycline would quickly clear it up. If these men were
hospital they could be certainly cured… Behind her, the
door opened.

She turned, in some strange way anger replacing her fear.
the doorway was Goldtooth, behind him an even larger
an. She guessed he was the one who had helped carry her.
'These men are ill!' she snapped. 'They need immediate
ospital care.'

Goldtooth smiled unpleasantly. 'I'm afraid that's not pos-
ble. However, I have food here. You may feed them if you
ish.' The man behind him moved into the room and put a
rge pan of something on the floor.

'I can't treat them here! And if I'm not back soon, my
iends will come for me.'

'I rather suspect they would have been here before if they
new where you were. Anyway, that is a chance I am will-
g to take.'

'These men are here illegally, aren't they?'

He shrugged. 'Workers are needed everywhere. Unfor-
nately, these seem to have brought their own illness with
em.'

She couldn't believe his calmness. 'You know they're
oing to die if they don't have treatment? Even worse, they
uld start an epidemic.'

Obviously he didn't want to think about that. His previous
ood temper disappeared. 'Feed them if you wish,' he
arled. 'I have arrangements to make. This place is no
nger any use to us. We'll have to move out.'

'What about me?' She didn't mean to ask the question—
showed fear. But somehow it had slipped out.

'You know nothing. When we go we'll release you.'

She didn't believe him. But the door shut before she could
y anything.

The pan contained some kind of mealie porridge. It was
arm and presumably nourishing, and she tried to spoon

some of it into the mouths of the sick men. They didn'
seem very interested so she fetched them water.

The man she thought the most sick moaned. She felt h
forehead, took his pulse, listened to his breathing. This ma
was going to die—soon! She ran to the door, pounded
with her fist, then kicked it. 'There's a man here, dying
she screamed.

Nothing happened. When she stopped it struck her ho
silent the place was. No sound of traffic or anything.
London that was *very* unusual. She could die here and r
one would know.

She slumped by the door. Suddenly her head hurt.
struck her that since she'd regained consciousness she
been kept active by adrenaline. She'd seen this kind of h
peractivity in accident victims before. But it soon passed.
was passing for her now. She felt sick. Then she felt tire
If she closed her eyes for a minute, perhaps she'd feel bett

She awoke. Somehow she knew she'd slept for qui
some time. Her eyes felt sticky, her body cold and crampe
In front of her the door was opening. She didn't really ca
She wasn't even surprised when James was the first ma
through it.

'Delyth, are you all right?' Even in her confused state sl
could tell there was a world of pain and anxiety in his voic
He does care a bit about me, she thought as he stooped l
her side.

'Just a bump on the head,' she said. 'And I think n
wrist is broken.' There was so much she wanted to say l
him, but her doctor's training took over. There were thin
she had to say. 'James, I think these men have bubor
plague. They need—'

'I know what they've got,' he said. 'Relax now. It's a
being taken care of.' She looked behind him. The room w
filling with men dressed in white overalls and masks. Th

were bending over her patients. They weren't her patients now—she didn't need to take charge. Throwing her arms around him, she collapsed, weeping, on his shoulder.

For a while he just held her. But then she felt slightly better, and he gave her a quick examination. 'Just your head and wrist? Sure there're no other injuries, nothing broken, no odd pains?'

I was walking around before you came.'

He flicked a torch from his pocket and shone it into her eyes. 'I don't think you're concussed,' he said, 'but we'll see.'

Behind him there was a rattle and two trolleys were wheeled into the room. One stopped by her. 'She seems OK,' James said, and took her shoulders as a paramedic took her thighs.

'There're other people who need attention before…' she started. Then she was gently lifted onto the trolley.

'You're not the doctor now—I am,' James said with some heat. 'I take the decisions. You've done enough. Now you're going to hospital. Delyth, why didn't you tell me what you were doing? I thought we were friends. I thought we could talk. You scared me.' He walked by her side as she was wheeled and carried through the dank corridors of the warehouse. There seemed to be a lot of people here. Policemen, as well as paramedics.

'We are friends,' she mumbled. 'James, you must tell me, how did you know where to find me?'

He squeezed her hand. 'I turned detective. There's been a lot happened you don't know about.'

'But I want to know. I need to—'

'I'll be in to see you later. Just take it easy. You're a patient now, not a doctor.'

He was friendly, but his face gave as little away as ever. Or did it? Was there some pain there, some feeling over and above what she'd expect him to show for a colleague? She thought so. But, then, she knew she'd had a bad blow to the head. Perhaps it was affecting her judgement.

The street outside was busy. As well as ambulances, there were police vehicles and a public health van. There seemed to be an awful lot of people being efficient. She was lifted into an ambulance. 'I'll be in to see you when I can,' James said, 'but for the moment I'm afraid I'm needed here.'

'Come soon,' she said, and closed her eyes.

She wasn't taken to her own hospital. She found herself in a room on her own, with a nurse helping her to undress and wash and lending her a nightie. Then an older doctor came to see her and examined her thoroughly. He carried out all the tests that she would have done, gave her head a CT scan and X-rayed her wrist. 'A nasty bang to the skull,' he told her, 'but I don't think there'll be any lasting consequences. We'll strap up your wrist—it'll stop you working for a while. And I gather you've been near some rather nasty germs, but I doubt you're infected. However, we'll give you an injection which is certain to stop them getting a grip. Doxycycline, I think. Try to get some sleep.'

So she did try, but a question nagged at her. How had James found her? She thought of her desperate, panic-stricken attempt to send him a message. Had he received it? What a silly idea!

Next morning was odd. She knew she should have been at work, but was quite content just to lie in bed. She wasn't exactly in pain, though her head ached. She felt lethargic. Everything was too much trouble.

With one hand she picked at the breakfast that a nurse brought her. An earnest young doctor came to see her, introducing himself as Dr Myers. With a giggle she realised he was the same as her—a house officer. It was interesting to consider his bedside manner from the patient's point of view. Did he fill her with confidence?

'There's a message for you from the head of your firm,'
: told her. 'Dr Forrester. He says you're not to worry about
ork and he'll be in to see you this afternoon. And a Dr
wen will be in some time this morning.'

Her heart thudded for some reason which she didn't think
as to do with her condition.

Dr Myers went on, 'I'm doing my medical house job
)w, of course, but I'd like to do surgical with Dr
)rrester's firm next. Is there any chance of getting onto it,
you think?'

'You'll learn a lot,' she told him. 'You say this is a med-
al firm?'

'And how! You've caused all sorts of excitement. The
en you came in with are in a ward below. We've never
)me across anything like this before.'

'It is bubonic plague, isn't it?' she asked. 'How are they
l doing?'

He frowned, obviously not wanting to break patient con-
dentiality.

'Look,' she said, 'I've met them. I even tried to treat
em. If you like, they're my patients too.'

That decided him. 'I'm afraid one died last night. But
e're pumping doxycycline into the others—they should be
l right. We think we've caught them in time. It's an easy
sease to treat if you catch it in its early stages.'

After that she just lay there till James came at mid-
orning. Normally she would have felt excitement at seeing
m, and eagerness to know exactly what had happened, but
ere was still this feeling of lethargy.

He looked well. Obviously he'd been somewhere where
:'d needed to command attention. He wore a dark suit,
hite silk shirt, college tie. 'Who's trying to look important,
en?' she asked feebly.

He leaned over to kiss her on the cheek, then sat by the
:d. 'I've been meeting important people,' he told her.

'Medical people, public health people, police, even t
Home Office. You've really stirred things up, haven't you'

'Tell me. I still don't know really what happened.'

'Right. First of all, I've tried to keep you out of things.
take it the last thing you want is publicity. You don't wa
to appear in court, do you?'

'No! I couldn't stand it! What would my family think?'

'They might think they had a truly exceptional daughte
and sister. But that's by the way. You had a patient injure
in a fight. You weren't to know that he was also in the earl
stages of bubonic plague. The blood you took was teste
for blood gases, not anything infectious. Anyway, the pa
tient was an illegal immigrant, smuggled in by our frien
with the gold teeth. He got fed up with being confined in
cellar and tried to escape. That's when he was beaten u
Goldteeth found out which hospital he was in and came t
the ward and told him that if he didn't come back to th
warehouse, he'd be deported as an illegal immigrant. S
with help, he signed himself out. Then the plague got hir
as it had his friends. They must have been infected in the
own country. Goldteeth just didn't know what to do. He
now co-operating completely with the police. They've g
enough on him to lock him up for quite a stretch, withou
charging him with assault.'

It was a simple but sad story. But there was more sl
needed to know. 'How did you find me?' she asked.

He showed a touch of anger. 'It was pure chance, Delyt
These people can be desperate…violent. I just came on
the ward and you weren't there. I was a bit surprised so
asked Matt where you were. He said you'd wanted an afte
noon off for some reason. When I pressed him he thoug
you were concerned about a patient that had signed himse
out. So I looked for the patient's notes and discovered you'
been in touch with A and E about him. Then Matt told m

he'd seen you borrowing a nurse's uniform. I was getting worried.

'I found that you'd sent a blood sample for blood gases, and asked them for the fullest survey—for some reason I asked about diseases. When plague turned up in the results I informed Public Health and the police. They took it from there. It'll be a reasonably happy ending all round. The building will be fumigated, the men treated. Simple, really.'

She tried to concentrate. It wasn't simple, really. 'When do I get out of here?' she asked.

'Ah. You can't really go straight back on the ward. That head of yours isn't so good, and after the traumatic afternoon you had Mr Forrester thinks you ought to have some time off. A month, he thinks. And he's talking about counselling.'

'I don't need counselling! There's nothing wrong— Ow!' She tried to jerk forward. There definitely *was* something wrong with her head.

'When he was told that you were a house officer, the consultant in charge here thought a month off a good idea. So do I and, most important, so does Forrester. His decision, but I agree with it.'

'All right,' she said.

'I'm glad you're being reasonable. I'm going to France for a fortnight next week, and I wouldn't want to have to worry about you while I was away.'

'Very thoughtful of you,' she muttered. Why was he going to France? But there was still something else that was bothering her.

'All this trouble you went to,' she said, 'just because I wasn't on the ward. Why didn't you wait till I was obviously missing? I might have been shopping or something simple like that.'

He shrugged. 'It didn't feel like you. I knew something was wrong.'

She seized on his confession. 'You *knew* something was wrong. Matt wasn't worried, was he? Why should you be?'

'It was a good thing I did get worried,' he pointed out, slightly irritated.

'It was in the early afternoon, wasn't it?' She could tell the conversation was making him uncomfortable, but she didn't intend to relent.

'Yes, I think so. You weren't on the ward and I thought it odd.'

'James, when I was thrown into that cellar and I first came to, I was terrified. I didn't know what to do. So I thought of you, harder than I've ever thought of anything in my life before. I wanted you with me. It was early afternoon. And that's when you first worried about me.'

He smiled at her gently—which infuriated her. 'Your sixth sense again, Delyth. It was nothing like that. I was just concerned about a colleague. I would have done the same for anyone.'

'Are you sure about that?'

His answer was bland. 'I'm certain,' he said.

CHAPTER EIGHT

JAMES knew it was a tricky manoeuvre for a house officer to perform. Insertion of a central line into the jugular vein involved locating the needle and then the cannula just to the side of the carotid artery.

Carefully, Matt felt the pulse of the great neck artery with his left hand, then slid home the needle with his other hand, at an angle of 45 degrees. He was successful in finding the vein. Blood appeared in his syringe. As James watched, Matt withdrew his needle and then re-inserted a larger-bore needle. All was going according to plan. The next step was to introduce the guide wire. Matt slid the soft end first down the hollow needle, and carefully fed the wire into the vein. When about half of the wire was in the vein he removed the needle, nicked the skin at the entry point and threaded the dilator onto the wire. Then it was only a case of removing the dilator, threading on the cannula, making sure it was sterile and securing it.

'That was very good, Matt,' James said when they had looked at a chest X-ray and seen that the cannula was properly in place. 'I'll watch the next time you do it, but after that you'll be on your own. Remember, if you should accidentally hit the carotid artery—and one day you will—apply full pressure for five minutes.'

Their patient needed TNP—total parenteral nutrition. Because it was impossible for the man to take in sufficient food by mouth, it was being introduced straight into the bloodstream—in the heart. They had just fed a tube into the vein.

They walked back to the doctors' room for coffee. The

normally high-spirited Matt seemed unusually quiet. Jam
wondered what was wrong.

'I gather you've been to see Delyth,' Matt said after a
uncomfortable silence.

'Yes, I have. She looks well, but I agree that she shouldn
return to work for a while.'

There was another pause, then Matt said, 'I wonder if
could have a word with you some time?'

'I'm always ready to help, Matt. I've got a few minute
now.'

Matt looked even more uncomfortable. 'It's not anythir
medical. It's something personal. Could we meet outside th
hospital?'

Warily James said, 'We could if you wish. It's abo
Delyth, isn't it?'

'Yes, sir,' Matt said defiantly.

'Well, how about the Clubroom tonight? We could me
a bit earlier than usual—say about nine?'

'Thank you, that'd be fine, sir. Now I'd better get on.'

James watched him walk out of the room, his coffee u
touched. Matt had returned to formality, even though Jam
had told him that he was very happy to be addressed by h
first name—except when they were in front of a patie
together. James thought he knew what Matt was going
say. Now he had time to think about what he was going
answer. What was he going to answer?

James hadn't been to the Clubroom for a while, not sin
he'd stopped meeting Delyth there. He arrived early, wan
ing to sit, have a drink and collect his thoughts before Ma
came. When he walked into the room he felt a sudden jo
of disappointment. There would be no Delyth to meet hin
He hadn't realised how much he missed those shared la
evenings. Still, he reminded himself morosely, it had bee
his own decision. Why wasn't he happy with it?

He bought himself a beer, and got one for Matt, too. H

hought that Matt was going to ask him about his feelings
or Delyth, and he still didn't know what he was going to
ay. All afternoon he had pondered—and got nowhere. It
truck him that Delyth had affected him much, much more
han any of the women with whom he'd had brief and in-
onclusive affairs. Perhaps he was wrong about his feelings
or her? He shrugged angrily. That idea was ridiculous! He
new what he wanted.

Matt came into the room, looking both uncomfortable and
etermined. James remembered when he, too, had been in
ove. Not once but twice. For a moment he remembered the
xcitement, the exhilaration, the way love had coloured
verything he'd done. Life had been brighter then. Then he
emembered the unutterable sense of loss afterwards. He
asn't going through that pain again.

Matt walked over to his table. 'I got you a beer,' James
aid. 'Sit down and we'll talk about how you're in love with
elyth and you don't know what her feelings are towards
ou.'

Matt looked amazed. 'You know?' he asked.

'I'm not unobservant,' James said gently. 'I know you
ink a lot of her.'

Matt took a chair and drank from his beer. 'She started
a friend,' he said. 'In fact, she still is a friend. It's just
at…I feel bad that I paid no attention to her fears about
e missing patient. She tried to confide in me, but I paid
o attention. Then you spotted something was wrong and
ou found her.'

'It was sheer chance,' James assured him. Then he drank
me of his own beer and frowned. Why *had* he been so
set? Why had he gone to so much trouble? It so happened
at he had been completely right—but he might not have
en. The word 'intuition' crossed his mind but he rejected
Absolute rubbish!

'Anyway,' Matt said, 'I want to thank you. She is… T[
is, I want her to be…more than a friend now.'

'So you've come to warn me off her?' James asked flat[

The stark question upset Matt. James saw the blood r[
in his cheeks. 'Yes, I have,' Matt said. 'I think that fo[
senior member of hospital staff to take advantage of a ju[
member is…despicable.'

James felt the rage rising within him. How dared t[
young fool interfere with…? Did he think he was the o[
person in the world to have feelings? But fortunately [
managed to keep calm. After a silence he said, 'It must ha[
taken quite a lot of nerve to say that.'

It wasn't the answer the now pale Matt was expecti[
'It did,' he admitted.

Neither spoke for a while. Then James said, 'I'm not g[
ing to talk about my relationship with Delyth. She may t[
to you if she wishes.' With a secret ironic smile he reme[
bered that he had held back when he'd found that Del[
was a virgin. What would Matt think of that? Not, of cour[
that he intended to tell him.

He went on, 'I'll just tell you that I have as high [
opinion of her as you have. And I would never take adv[
tage of my senior position. Like you, I think it's despicabl[

Eagerly Matt asked, 'Then you're not interested in her[
that way, I mean?'

James drained his glass. He looked at Matt's bar[
touched beer and said with a grin, 'Your round, isn't it?[

Matt smiled tightly. 'I'll fetch you a beer,' he said. 'I[
give you time to think of your answer.'

James winced as Matt walked over to the bar. One d[
this young man would be a good doctor. He had the rig[
feeling for people. When he returned James said, 'I told y[
I wouldn't talk about my relationship with Delyth—tha[
up to her. I'll just use one quaint, stupid, old-fashion[

rd. With her my behaviour will be honourable. D'you
ieve me?'

'Yes,' said Matt after a pause. There was another silence
1 then he went on, 'I hope I'll be like you when I get
ler.'

'How's that?' asked James, genuinely curious.

'Clever,' said Matt.

don't think I really like being a patient,' Delyth said.
She felt at a disadvantage, looking up at Michael
rrester, the consultant who was head of her firm. Usually
y stood side by side, either in white coats, looking down
a patient in bed, or in theatre greens. Now he was elegant
a grey pinstripe three-piece suit and she was in a floral
htie. It just wasn't right.

'I can understand that,' he replied urbanely, 'but perhaps
; good for all of us to see things from the other side, as
vere.'

She wondered how long it had been since he'd been made
lie in bed when he'd known there was nothing wrong
h him, but she wisely said nothing.

'I'm pleased to see you making such good progress, such
apid recovery,' he added.

This was her chance. 'I feel much better now,' she rushed
'and I'd really like to start work on the ward again soon.
now my wrist will make things difficult but I could do
ne things. I'm sorry if I acted a bit precipitately but—'

He raised his hand to stop her. 'What you did was in
ne ways admirable.' He fetched a chair to sit beside her.
happily, she realised she was in for a long talk.
nsultants didn't normally sit in chairs by bedsides.

'I've been making a few enquiries about you,' he went
when he had made himself comfortable. 'With the pres-
e of work, too often we don't know enough about the
ung doctors who come onto our wards. Perhaps we

should. I've been told that you worked extremely hard
your degree—as most medical students do. But after
exams most of them took a much-needed holiday. Y
didn't. Instead, you worked long hours at a cottage hospi
near your home, with your local GP—a Dr Alun Robert

That was true. 'He encouraged me to apply for medi
school,' she explained. 'And he helped me in the cour
When I got the chance to do something for him—'

'So you didn't have a holiday,' he interrupted. 'Delyt|
don't know what people have been saying to you. But c
thing must be emphasised. You made a serious error
judgement. As it happens, the consequences haven't b
too bad. They could have been disastrous. The least y
should have done was tell people what you were thinki
of. Isn't it hammered into you when you first get on a wa
Everything is written down. You make certain that ot|
people know what you are doing.'

'I suppose so,' she mumbled.

He put a crumpled envelope on the table by her bed, a
motioned for her to open it. Out of it dropped ten pou
coins.

'A patient called Birdie Jones came to my clinic yest
day,' he said. 'He asked especially to see you. When I s
you weren't available, he asked me to give you this. In ti
I got him to tell me why.'

'It was my money. I can do what I like with it,' s
pointed out resentfully.

'True. And I must say I took to young Birdie. But w|
I'm saying is that as doctors we must be caring and co
passionate—the patient is always a human being, not a ca
But you cannot interfere too much with patients' lives. C
job is a medical one. That is all we have time for. I thi
you're in danger of getting too close, even too involved, a
I think it's dangerous. You're overtired. So I'm prescribi
rest for another three weeks. Is that all right?'

'I suppose so,' she mumbled. She knew she didn't have uch choice.

'Good. Now, we can take it that you don't have plague. 's an unpleasant disease, but laughably easy to treat if ught early enough. Your head and wrist are coming along asonably well. I know you could go home—I've heard out your family from Dr Owen. But I've got another idea. ly brother has a farmhouse in the south of France which :'s converted so that people can stay there. A lot of med-al staff go there—we have a relationship with a hospital earby. In fact, Dr Owen is going there next weekend for a rtnight. He's going to work. I want you to go with him d rest.'

She looked up, bewildered. 'Have you asked him?' she ked.

'No, but I'm sure he'd be only too pleased to take you ith him. Someone for him to talk to on the journey.'

It struck her that perhaps Mr Forrester had been right. He ould know a little more about the young doctors who me onto his ward. Then he wouldn't have suggested this.

'I think a fortnight in a warmer climate will be good for u,' he went on. 'And let me make one thing clear. You're t coming back onto my firm until I think you're ready.'

'I'd love to go,' she said, 'if you're sure Dr Owen ouldn't mind taking me.'

She wondered why she was so keen to go. Hadn't James ade it clear that there was no future for them together?

'ithout Delyth the ward's paperwork was piling up. That ternoon Matt was sitting in the doctors' room, patiently orking his way through the usual mass of forms. They had be done so he was doing them. But they were tedious! James had called in for the notes on a patient he was due operate on the next day. He saw Matt gloomily at work,

and offered to help for half an hour. The two worked to
gether in companionable silence.

The door opened and Mr Forrester peered inside. 'Ju
been to see Delyth,' he said. 'She's making excellent pro
gress. I've made a couple of phone calls and we've got
replacement for her for the next two weeks. James, I kno
you're driving down to Villeneuf next Sunday. I thought
a good idea if Delyth went as well to recuperate. You don
mind taking her, do you?'

After a moment's thought James said, 'If she's agreeabl
I've hired a big car.'

'That's settled, then.' The consultant left.

James looked at Matt and shrugged. 'Not my idea,' h
said.

'I know. You can bring me a bottle of wine back.'

Megan had returned to London by train after a week a
home. Her first trip out was to visit her injured sister.

'So I'm going to France with him,' Delyth told Mega
'D'you think that's a good idea?'

She wriggled inside her dressing-gown. She was gettin
tired of sitting around, doing nothing. She'd tried to wri
a letter home, but had given up. Between them, she an
Megan had decided that she wouldn't tell their parents abo
what had happened. They would only have worried. And
was hard to write a letter home without mentioning that sh
was in hospital herself.

'I'm not sure going away with James Owen is a goo
idea,' Megan said. 'Though the stay in France sounds fine

'He won't be…pushy or anything like that.'

'I know,' Megan said sharply. 'I can tell from his fac
That's the least of my worries. It's not his actions I'm wo
ried about, it's your feelings. You've never been like th
before. I think you're pushing yourself into a situation that'

urt you. And I don't know why. Anyway, what about this
oung doctor you were seeing?'

Delyth sighed. She didn't feel happy about the way she
ad treated Matt, though she had tried to make her feelings
lear to him.

'He came to see me, and he was ever so sweet. But I
ealised that I was just using him to try and forget James.
. wasn't fair on him. So I told him that I liked him a lot
nd hoped we'd still be friends, but that would be all.'

'I'll bet he loved that. What did he say?'

'He was upset, but he took it very well. Said I'd had a
asty shock…needed to recuperate…this wasn't the time to
nake decisions. We could talk when I was fully better and
ertainly he wouldn't force himself on me.'

'Sounds a good sort,' announced Megan, chewing on one
f the grapes she'd brought. 'Are you sure you want to get
d of him?'

'I wish he'd got angry,' Delyth confessed. 'He was en-
tled to, and I could have dealt with that better. I found
nyself liking and admiring him even more.'

'But not loving him?'

'No, not loving him.'

Megan scowled, then stood and limped over to help her-
elf to more grapes. 'I thought I'd got you settled,' she said
ccusingly. 'Now you've changed your mind and I have to
arry on worrying. You said you knew James wasn't for
ou. You were going to give him up and remain friends.
ine, I thought, very civilised, very sensible. He'd made his
osition clear—he couldn't have been more obvious. But
ow you're thinking there's some hope for you after all. I'm
ght, aren't I?'

'Well, perhaps I am just a bit,' Delyth admitted.

'Why? I know he drove me home but, other than that,
as he given you any reason to think that he wants a lasting

relationship with you? Is it just because he rode in to sav
you from danger, like some knight on a big white horse?'

'He thinks of me as a friend and a colleague,' Dely
cried. 'He likes me.'

'And that's all. But you know better than him what he
thinking.'

Delyth remembered her terrified silent plea when she
been locked in the cellar. He had responded to that. No ov
else had worried—only James had heard her and come
seek her out.

'I don't know what he wants,' she said. 'He's had a ha
life. I know there's a black side to his soul but I think l
might improve.'

Megan shook her head despairingly. 'Six sisters are ar
ists. And the single scientist amongst us is the one refusin
to listen to logic. Delyth, you worry me! You're throwir
yourself at this man! He's told you he wouldn't mind bein
your lover—something temporary. He's made that ve
clear. You can't blame him if he takes advantage of wh
you're offering him.'

' I'm not offering him anything,' Delyth said. 'We're ju
travelling to France together and we should enjoy ead
other's company on the way. That's all. Anyway, wouldr
you like James as a brother-in-law?'

'I give up,' Megan said.

But when James came to see Delyth again she was mu
more uncertain. Perhaps Megan was right. Perhaps she w
making a serious error of judgement. James was friendl
but nothing more. On Saturday she was to return to tl
residence by taxi, pack, then get to bed early. 'Rememb
how tiring a few days in bed can be,' he told her. 'You'
not going to be half as strong as you think.'

'I just want to get out of this ward. Doing nothing
driving me mad.'

'You'll be doing something on Sunday,' he told her drily. 'I want you up at half past four in the morning. We're catching the ferry from Portsmouth at half past seven.'

'I've never had any problem getting out of bed.'

'D'you know what clothes to take? It'll be warmer than England, but we're going to Aquitaine, which means the watery district, so it can pour down.'

'I've been reading this book about the area. I know what to take. James, I'm really looking forward to this. And, let's be clear, I want to pay my way. I'm not going to—'

'It's all been taken care of,' he told her. 'But you'll need to spend something when you're there. If you give me a cheque for a hundred pounds I'll get you some francs and arrange some traveller's cheques. Anything else I can get for you?'

As in everything he did, he was efficient and thoughtful. But he wasn't loving. He treated her like any friend and she felt a tiny bit hurt. But they were going to be so much together. Perhaps love between them would suddenly develop. If it didn't...her future looked bleak.

Even though James had warned her, she was surprised at how weak she had become. She shouldn't have been surprised. She remembered big, strong men who couldn't believe how powerless they were after two or three weeks' bed rest. She now had a fresh, lighter dressing on her wrist. It was still uncomfortable but she could do most things with it.

Matt came in a taxi to fetch her. She felt grateful, and slightly tearful at this. But he was nothing but friendly and concerned. There were no reproaches. He helped her to her room, fetched her the inevitable mug of tea and went to find her cases from the store down the corridor.

'You'll want a bit of time to yourself,' he said. 'You'll

need to rest after packing. But you know my room—shou
if there's anything at all I can do.'

'Thanks, Matt, you're a real friend.'

Packing didn't take long. There were few decisions—
she'd carefully made a list while lying in bed. Then sh
discovered Matt had been right. She did want time to her
self. She wasn't interested in gossip about the ward or work
She decided to lie on her bed.

For a moment there was a quick feeling of panic. Thi
was just not like her. She felt remote, detached, not con
cerned with things she knew should concern her. She won
dered about her parents. Megan had said that she woul
write to them, saying that Delyth was very busy and ha
been offered the chance to observe in a hospital in France
This was almost true. But Delyth didn't feel the guilt sh
would have expected at half deceiving them.

Still in her dreamlike state, she checked her packing
looked at the medication she'd been left, set the alarm an
decided to sleep. She knew she'd have no difficulty wakin
as she was accustomed to early rising.

It was still dark at half past four. She showered, dresse
in the tracksuit that James had suggested, packed he
nightie, washbag and other things in the little bag he ha
told her she was to take on board. Then she waited till h
knocked softly on the door. He had insisted that she didn'
try to carry her cases down.

She thrilled to see him. Like her he was dressed for com
fort, in cords and a loose sweater. She felt they were t
share an adventure, at the beginning of something that migh
be more than a mere journey. For a second, as he first looke
at her, she thought that he felt the same way. But perhap
it was just a friendly smile.

They went downstairs to his hired car, a burgundy
coloured Discovery, a bit smaller and more modern tha
Megan's great vehicle. In the back was a pile of papers an

quipment he was taking to the French hospital. He helped
er up onto her seat.

The London traffic was very quiet at this time of the
norning. They threaded their way easily through the centre
nd were soon on the M 3 at a steady seventy miles an hour.
he didn't sleep, as she had done the last time he'd driven
er. She wanted to experience every moment of the day.

There weren't too many cars driving their way, but the
ncoming vehicles were now in one long procession. 'Com-
nuters,' he told her. 'Coming in for their daily boring work.
sn't it exciting to be escaping, going the other way?'

He'd caught her mood exactly. 'It's like when we used
o drive off on our holidays together,' she told him. 'It's
tarting a journey, watching the world come to life as dawn
reaks. It's magic.'

They didn't talk much after that, being content to sit qui-
tly. Instead he fumbled in his pocket and clicked in a tape.
he soft voice of Lena Horne filled the car, singing love
ongs.

'That's one of my favourites,' she told him. 'We have
astes in common.'

He smiled gently. 'I do like it,' he said. 'But I must con-
ess I phoned Megan and asked her what music you liked.
 bought this tape specially for you.'

'I see,' she said. She wondered what to make of that.

The morning was grey at first, but then the sun made a
veak appearance. Eventually they swung off the motorway
nd onto the coast road, and then parked in the queue for
ne ferry at Portsmouth. Now she *did* feel she was going on
oliday.

Ahead of them were two giant white ships, impossibly
igh. There was the screaming of gulls. They were directed
xpertly from queue to queue, then up a rattling steel ramp
o the hold. There was the glimpse of water far below, and

then they were packed in tightly with the other cars. Carefully, they climbed out.

As Delyth wriggled past the other cars, at James's suggestion carrying a coat and her little bag, it struck her that she hadn't left so many arrangements to another person since she was a little child. Why had she so much faith in James's decisions? It seemed as if she knew that everything he wanted she would want, too.

'Travelling excites me,' he told her, and she knew it. She could tell by the eagerness of his step and the brightness of his eye. 'We're six hours on this ship. I thought you might like to stay on deck as we sail, have a quick breakfast and then sleep.'

'Whatever you think,' she assured him. 'It sounds wonderful to me.' There were quite a few sets of stairs until they got to where they could be in the open air. Her legs were weak and he had to help her.

'When we get to Villeneuf I'll give you a set of graded exercises,' he told her. 'After a fortnight you'll be as good as new. Just don't try to do too much.'

'No, Doctor,' she said with mock humility, and he turned and grinned at her.

The great ship hummed. They saw the water boiling far below them as slowly and gracefully they backed out of their berth and set off down the Solent. Delyth decided she had been too long in hospital, and was eager for new sights. They stood silently together, watching the grey sleekness of a destroyer, the vastness of an aircraft carrier, the amazing rigging of Nelson's *Victory*. They smelled the sea, listened again to the screaming of the gulls. Then they passed a tiny fort in the water and they were out on the open sea.

'Fancy some breakfast?' James asked, and she realised she was indeed hungry. When she moved away from the rail she staggered a little, and instantly his arm was around her. It was only for support, and for a moment she leaned against him. It was very comforting.

Then she moved away. It was good of him to offer her this lift. She wouldn't repay his kindness by showing herself to be expecting a relationship that he didn't want. But if he *did* find that he wanted it...

In the café he found her a table by the window and fetched them both a breakfast tray. She wasn't hungry—she was ravenous. Usually she had a good appetite, but had reacted to life as a hospital patient by eating less than usual. Now, after the sea air, she tucked into the cereal, bacon and egg that he had brought her. It was so satisfying. And then...

'You're tired,' he told her. He was right—she was exhausted. But she wasn't going to admit it.

'I am not tired,' she told him, then contradicted herself by yawning hugely.

'Don't worry, I've got everything planned. Come on down to our cabin.'

'Our cabin?' she asked. This was interesting.

'Your cabin, then. For every double ticket there's a cabin. You're lucky, yours is an outside one.'

She followed him down more stairs and along long corridors. The humming of the ship's engines grew louder. Now she knew she was tired. The prospect of bed was inviting. Eventually he checked the number on a door and opened it to show her into a tiny cabin.

There were two berths, one on top of the other. There was a ladder and a place to hang coats. Another door opened into an equally tiny shower room. It all seemed wonderfully cosy.

'Bed,' he suggested. 'I'll give you a knock three quarters of an hour before we dock. That'll give you time for a shower and a sandwich.'

She frowned. 'What about you? You need your sleep too.'

'I'll catch a couple of hours in a reclining chair. They're very comfortable. I'm a doctor, I can sleep anywhere.'

'No.' She was firm. 'We're colleagues. You can have the top bunk. I'll be unhappy if you don't. Besides, you've got a long way to drive and you shouldn't be tired. You've got a precious cargo. Me.'

He looked down at her sitting on the lower bunk. 'Yes,' he agreed, 'I have a precious cargo. OK, you go to bed and I promise to come back in an hour or so.'

'Take the key,' she told him.

When he'd gone she changed into her nightie and slipped between the cool sheets. The engine's hum was hypnotic. She had intended to think about a few things but instead, she slept at once.

She awoke to the smell of coffee. James was offering her a plastic cup. 'We'll be there soon,' he said. 'Drink this and then have a shower.'

She blinked. 'Have I been asleep all this time?'

'Sleeping like a baby. I came in after an hour and tiptoed round, but I don't think a full force gale would have woken you. So I also slept.'

Delyth took the coffee, noticing that his hair was wet. 'I've just had a shower myself,' he told her. 'Now, I'll leave you for twenty minutes and then we'll watch the ship dock.'

After the shower she felt refreshed, full of excitement, eager for the next part of the journey. He collected her and they had a swift sandwich in the cafeteria, then just had time to watch the ferry slide neatly into what seemed an impossibly small space. There was the reverse scramble to get in the car, the wait which now seemed longer and then the clanking out into daylight.

They were in France! She saw signs telling them to drive on the right, and they followed other, largely British cars. The houses seemed different, the fields looked different, even the weather felt different. She glanced at him, driving confidently, and saw that he, too, was enjoying himself. 'Landfall,' he told her. 'The start of something new. Always exciting, isn't it?'

'Yes,' she agreed, 'an exciting start of something new.'

Their route took them across Normandy to the *autoroute* at Tours. From there they would curve down across the west of France. For the first stage of the journey they were both content to watch and say little. After they'd joined the *autoroute* he drove for about thirty miles and then stopped.

'I don't believe in driving for too long,' he told her. 'We'll stretch our legs, have a drink.' He took her for a walk around. French motorway stops were superior to English ones, she thought. Not as busy, better landscaped and somehow different. She enjoyed herself, and when they started the drive again she was invigorated. She wanted something new now.

He handed her a bag. 'Pick a tape,' he urged her. 'Music for gentle driving.'

'No. If you don't mind, I'd rather talk to you.'

'Talk about anything you like,' he invited. 'I'm a good listener.'

'I know you are. You're a good talker, too, but recently you've been gentle with me. You've not wanted to push me too hard because of the injury to my head. True?'

He was silent a moment and then said, 'Yes, that's true, Delyth.'

'Well, I'm now declaring myself officially well. There are a couple of things I want to ask you, and I also want to tell you something.' She paused. 'You know I've made a statement to the police about what happened in the warehouse?'

'Yes. In fact, I've seen some of it.'

'Good. Apart from that, everyone has been tiptoeing round me, not wanting to ask questions in case I was upset.

Even the policewoman was extra nice to me. I felt like an invalid. I was even offered counselling!'

'You should have accepted,' he told her. 'There are people who haven't been able to get back to work after suffering what you did.'

'Well, I'm tougher than them. And now I want to talk about what happened.'

For a moment he took his eyes off the road to glance at her. 'Are you sure that's a good idea?'

'It's an excellent idea. And it's you that's going to be cross-examined, not me. I've asked you about it once. Now I want more details.' She took a breath. 'We've established that I did something stupid chasing after that man, especially not telling anyone what I was doing. When I was gone Matt, who cares for me a lot, didn't worry at all. Why should he? But you did. Why should you, a very busy doctor, suddenly decide that I might be in danger, go to quite considerable trouble to find out where I'd gone, even contact the police? On the face of it, it doesn't seem necessary.'

'It was necessary,' he pointed out, 'and the more I enquired the more certain I became.'

'But why did you worry in the first place?'

He laughed. 'I know where you're going, Delyth. You think this sixth sense of yours contacted me. I thought it only told you when people were ill.'

She ignored his laughter. She thought it sounded slightly forced. 'That's true,' she said. 'But I was terrified, more than I've ever been in my life before. So I lay there and I tried to talk to you. And after I tried I felt better, and when you turned up in the cellar I wasn't really surprised.'

He took a hand off the wheel and laid it on hers. 'Yours is one account,' he said. 'Another is that, as you said, you were terrified. You were disorientated, not capable of rational thought. In that state the mind seizes any comfort. Sorry, Delyth, that's all there is to it.'

'Possibly,' she said. 'What about your actions, then?'

He shrugged. 'Matt didn't worry because he'd just seen you. I came along and realised your actions were a bit unusual. And quickly I found out enough to be very suspicious.'

She had to admit that what he said was plausible. She wondered if it was true.

They drove on without speaking further. Now they were well into France she thought there was a difference in the weather, even in the quality of the light. She was enjoying herself, but he misjudged her silence.

'I'm sorry to doubt your theories,' he said, 'but I've always been a rationalist. Still, we're good friends and I think we can agree to differ. Tell me what else you wanted to talk about. I'll talk about anything.'

'D'you mean that?'

'Any subject at all.'

'Then I want you to tell me about the two girls you fell in love with.' Delyth looked at him, and saw his face seem to turn to stone. 'Please,' she hurried on, 'don't talk if you don't want to. I don't want to pry.'

After a silence he said, 'Nobody has ever tried to talk to me about either of them. I mean really talk. I don't know if I can.'

'Talking can be good. Aren't you the man who's in favour of counselling?'

She saw a tiny smile. 'You're a tough one to fight with,' he said. 'Do you talk? Do you talk about me?'

'To a certain extent. I talk to Megan most, even though we're not at all alike. She likes you a lot.'

'I'll bet that's not all.'

'No,' she said cautiously. 'She says there's something in your face that's hidden. She thinks you might hurt me, even though you don't want to.'

'Do you think I might hurt you?'

'I think you could,' she said simply. 'I know there's a black side to you. But that night when you...when we nearly...I was very upset at the time. But afterwards I thought a lot of you because of it.'

'It wasn't one of the best nights of my life,' he growled.

He had been slowing down, now he turned into an *aire de repos*. She'd noticed these and thought they were a really good idea. They weren't proper motorway service stations. There were no shops or petrol pumps. Just a tiny park. There was a toilet block, a landscaped area, rustic tables in the shade. She'd seen people picnicking at them. Now James parked. 'We'll have a little rest,' he said.

She followed him as he walked up a bank and rounded a clump of trees. In a little hollow was a table. They sat opposite each other. Behind them was a vast green field, the spire of a church beyond that. The hum of traffic was muted and they seemed entirely alone.

He put his elbows on the table, then reached over and took her clasped hands, holding them loosely between his.

'Erin and then Hilary,' he said.

'With Erin, we were together so long that we didn't realise what was happening to us. Love grew slowly. We had so much else to think about at work. We had such a lot in common, suffering through the last two years of medical school and finals. Then we were both doctors. The world was in front of us. We had wild plans for when we finished our house officers' jobs. Our love for each other was part of everything we did. And she died. You've no idea what it's like—to wake up morning after morning, expecting to find a head on the pillow beside you and it's not there. No idea what it's like to think you're clawing your way out of a nightmare, and then to wake to find it's true.'

The terrible thing was his voice. There was no trace of emotion, no indication of the torment he must have felt— must be still feeling. He spoke softly, reflectively, as if these

ings had happened to someone else. 'And Hilary?' she
prompted.

'That was different to start with. She was a bit older than
me, had been hurt in a previous relationship. We were both
wary. But things grew. I found myself relaxing, thinking
that I could be happy again. And in time I was happy—we
both were. But we were content with what we had. We
didn't make any plans.'

He paused, and she thought he didn't want to go on. But
then he said, 'I remember once, when I was delivering a
baby, talking to the mother. It was her second child. The
first was happy and loved, this second one was planned and
all was going well. But she told me, before we gave her an
epidural, that with the pangs of the second baby all the
memories of pain from the first birth came flooding back.
It was like that when Hilary was knocked down. I'd forgotten the pain of loss. It came flooding back. But I knew
there'd be no end to it, no baby for me. She was bound to
die.'

She tried in vain to imagine how he must have felt—the
pain, the sheer horror. 'How did you manage?' she asked.
'How did you just…carry on?'

'It wasn't easy. I ran, sometimes twice a day. Exhausting
myself, pushing myself to the limit physically. It helped.
Running still helps me cope with things.'

Delyth wrestled with wildly different emotions. First there
was an overwhelming pity for him. Why should such a good
man have to suffer so much agony? And then there was a
deep feeling of frustration. He was wrong! She asked, 'So
you're not going to fall in love again?'

He didn't reply with the same assurance as he had in the
past. He frowned, as if he were hearing the words he was
using for the first time, as if he were convincing himself as
well as her. 'Why should I, Delyth? I have a happy, fulfilling
life. From time to time I meet girls who like my company

but don't want commitment. I won't hurt anybody. I would say it's a pretty useful arrangement, wouldn't you?'

'If it makes you happy,' she agreed. 'Are you trying to persuade me or yourself?'

He laughed, a little uneasily. 'You're too shrewd.' His voice altered, and he reached over to touch her cheek. 'But if I ever did want another long-term commitment, Delyth, it would be with someone like you.'

'I suppose that's a start.'

Did he know how deliriously happy he'd just made her?

CHAPTER NINE

THEY decided not to stop at a hotel. Delyth knew James was happy driving, and she urged him to press on. He stopped to make a quick telephone call to say they'd arrive late. Then he reclined her seat, and she dozed as they passed through the sea of great lights that was Bordeaux. Then it was into the dark along another *autoroute*.

It started to rain. 'This is Aquitaine,' he told her. 'What d'you expect?' She rather liked the way the rain rattled on the roof, and once or twice the interior of the car was lit by white sheet lightning. There was the distant rumble of thunder. James drove more slowly on the wet roads.

Then the rain stopped, and they turned off the *autoroute*, drove through a large village and into the darkness again. Only occasional lights on the distant hills showed any sign of civilisation. They turned onto a yet smaller road, and he stopped to read instructions by the navigation light. By now she was very tired, and she wondered how he felt. He looked as if he'd be happy enough to go on for ever!

Then he turned the wheel, the car lurched and there was the crunch of gravel. He stopped. 'We've arrived,' he said.

Exhausted, she stumbled out of the car, helped by an unseen hand. She was led inside what was called the barn. She had a vague impression of size, of old beams, old furniture. She sat at a great table. A kindly couple, Val and Tom, greeted her and gave her a sandwich and a cup of cocoa. They were her host and hostess. Tom looked like his brother Michael Forrester.

James sat opposite her. She wondered how he had driven so long without showing fatigue. Apart from little lines

149

round his eyes he looked as fresh as he had that morning
He smiled at her. 'You're tired,' he said, stating the obvious

Her cases were fetched and she was led to a tiny bedroom
and shown the bathroom next door. What if she had slep
on the journey? She would sleep some more. Within a min
ute she was in bed—a double, she noticed. Within two
minutes she was asleep.

Next morning was different. She awoke refreshed, excited
even. This stay was going to be some kind of an adventure
The memory of her fatigue the day before suggested to her
that she wasn't as strong as she used to be, but she'd im
prove. She had a fortnight—living next to James.

It was warmer than England. The sun shone through red
checked curtains. She looked around her room and saw sim
ple pine furniture, her case opened and abandoned on a
stool. There was a door into the barn proper, French win
dows opening to the sun.

There was a knock on the door. A little girl, aged abou
nine, appeared, carrying a steaming mug. She looked a
Delyth doubtfully. 'French people have coffee for break
fast,' she said. 'But my Dad said it's uncivilised and he
thought you'd prefer tea.'

'He's right,' Delyth said, reaching happily for the mug
'I'm Delyth. What's your name?'

'Delyth's a funny name. I'm called Ruth. If you want to
get up and put on your dressing-gown you could drink you
tea on the terrace. Other people are out there.'

It seemed a good idea. She rummaged in her case for a
robe, then followed Ruth out of the French windows. Tha
special sun, found only in the south, warmed her at once
In front of her was a path, a parapet and beyond it a sweep
of fields. She turned right to where she could hear voices
and there was the terrace, set with white metal tables and
chairs, and beyond it an incredibly blue pool. Everywhere

here were flowerpots, glowing with the reds of fuchsias and geraniums.

A little group of people were sitting together—Val and Tom, a couple of middle-aged smiling men and James. They stood as she approached. 'I think I'm going to enjoy myself here,' she said.

On the table was a plate for her, a choice between crusty bread or croissants, pots of tea and coffee. She was introduced to the two men, Alan and Claude, who were watercolourists, having three weeks' holiday. 'We've been coming here for five years now,' Claude told her. 'I'd retire here if I could.'

Breakfast apparently was usually a leisurely affair. There was another guest, a middle-aged lady called Marie Brown, who had left early to go for a walk. But the others sat and talked, in no great hurry.

After her mug of tea she decided to change to coffee. It was real French coffee, strong and black. 'This must be a better heart stimulant than adrenaline,' she told James.

It was the second day she'd done it. She was getting used to sitting opposite him at breakfast. She liked it. They felt comfortable together. 'It's good for you,' he told her. 'And I know you've got a heart like a horse. Did you sleep well?'

'Wonderfully well.' She looked at the hills around them. 'And this place is so beautiful. I want to see what's behind those hills. Look, there's a village perched right on the crest over there.'

He smiled at her enthusiasm. 'I'd like to see around myself. When I'm not working we'll explore together. But first I've got to get to the hospital. See you at suppertime.'

Only then did she notice that he was in semi-formal dress. A tie was looped loosely round the neck of his white shirt, there was a blazer on the chair behind him, a briefcase by his side. She'd almost forgotten he was here to work.

'At suppertime, then,' she said, feeling rather neglected
She wanted him to herself.

He must have noticed her disappointment. 'Val and Tom
will show you round,' he said. 'You still need to rest, you
know.'

'I'll show Delyth round,' a small but fierce voice butted
in. It was Ruth.

'Of course you will. She'll like that,' James said. He
stood, rested his hand on her shoulder a minute, then walked
decisively to his car.

Val drew her chair closer. 'You're convalescing,' she told
Delyth. 'Take things gently for a fortnight. I've heard a bit
of what you've been through, and my dear brother-in-law
isn't usually very easy on his younger staff. When you've
had another coffee I'll show you around the building. Then
why don't you sunbathe for a while?'

Sunbathe? How long had it been since she'd had a chance
just to sit in the sun? It had been years! 'I'd like that,' she
said.

'Good. Have you brought any sunblock?'

Delyth looked at her, amazed. 'I never thought of that.'

'I'll lend you some. And a straw hat. Don't let it fool you
around here. It might be nice now, but the weather can be
a killer.'

She loved Les Cabines. Val, Ruth and Tom lived in a
house on one side, the rest of them in a vast converted barn.
On the ground floor there was a kitchen, a central dining
area with one long oak table, bookshelves against the white
roughcast walls. There were five bedrooms and bathrooms.
Two open staircases led up to a large room with a polished
floor and different conversation areas.

'We want guests to treat the place as their own,' Val said.
'In the kitchen there's always bread, fruit, wine, and you
can make your own coffee or tea. Breakfast and lunch are

argely serve-yourself, but we like to have a big meal to-
ether at suppertime.'

'Have you been here long?' Delyth asked.

'Six years now. We don't advertise any more, we get so
nany repeats. Michael said he'd put some money into the
riginal conversion if we'd keep some places for his medical
taff. The local hospital is pleased too. We've had quite a
ew medical students doing their elective here.'

For a minute Delyth felt a bit of a stick-in-the-mud. She
ad done her elective in the cottage hospital near home.
till, Alun had helped her so much, and she had learned a
ot.

Ruth had been skipping by their side, showing Delyth
hings she might have missed, obviously pleased to be help-
ng. 'Can I ask a question?' she asked Delyth.

'Of course you can.'

'Is Dr Owen your boyfriend?'

'Hush, dear,' chided her mother. 'You don't ask people
uestions like that.'

'Well, he seems very fond of her,' Ruth pointed out with
nexorable logic. 'I think he would have kissed her this
norning, but there were people watching so he just
queezed her shoulder.'

'Ruth, you don't say things like that.'

'It's all right, Val. Ruth, he's my boss, and I like him a
ot, but he's not my boyfriend.'

'I'd bet he'd like to be.'

'Ruth! You must not make personal remarks. Tell Delyth
ou're sorry!'

Delyth saw the little face crumple. 'It's all right,' she said
ently. 'There's no need to say you're sorry. In fact, we're
ery good friends indeed.'

This time it was Val who looked at her.

he had an easy day. She read, lolled by the poolside. Only
vhen she tried to swim a couple of lengths did she realise

how weak she was. There was a lunch of fruit and sala
with Val and Tom, and then she dozed on a lounger Va
made her pull into the shade. 'I told you the weather wa
deceptive,' she said, and when Delyth felt the heat in he
skin she realised this was true.

She'd packed a set of medical textbooks but, instead c
improving herself, she decided to read for pleasure. It wa
years since she'd done so. In the bookshelf she found
remembered joy from her childhood, Jane Austen's *Pria
and Prejudice*.

'It is a truth universally acknowledged, that a young ma
of good fortune, must be in want of a wife.' Hmm, Delyt
thought, but read on anyway.

Ruth seemed to have adopted her. She wasn't a nuisanc
but was ever ready to fetch fruit or a drink. 'You can shou
for me if you want anything,' she told Delyth. 'And wi
you tell me how to become a doctor?' Delyth promised sh
would.

James came back earlier than expected. She sat up on he
lounger to greet him, not really surprised at the joy his pres
ence brought her. Then she remembered the keen eyes c
Ruth, and tried not to be too obvious. 'Had a good day'
she asked.

'Very good. It's a super little hospital. But yesterday i
taking its toll so I came back early. That pool looks good
His eyes moved down to her, now clad in shorts and T-shir
'So do you,' he added softly, and she blushed.

Before she could say anything more he went to his roon
then came out in shorts and a towel, and dived in the poo
He was a good swimmer, fast but not too splashy.

As Delyth watched him complete a dozen lengths sh
remembered what he'd said about this particular job. It wa
part of a scheme to introduce British doctors to Europea
hospitals to look at different methods of working and train

g, perhaps see if any ideas could be adapted. If Britain
came a full member of the European Community, there
ould be far more movement of doctors. This scheme
ould make it easier.

With a lithe movement he pulled himself out of the pool.
owelling himself, he came to sit by her. She had seen his
ar naked body before, of course, in the race and also…but
e wouldn't think of that. But each time she had been im-
essed by the tautness, the leanness, the sheer excitement
him. No fat, just long slender muscles, a faint dusting of
air on his chest and— A few drops of water from his rap-
ly towelled head splashed on her shoulders, and it felt as
they burned her. Concentrate!

'How was your day?' he asked.

'Easy. I tried to swim but I could only do two lengths.'

'You're still not fully fit,' he told her. 'Over the next
rtnight you must—'

'Thank you, Doctor.' She held up her hand to stop him.
now know how bad I am and will follow a sensible grad-
ated programme to restore myself to full health. I won't
ver-exert myself if you promise not to tell me not to.'

'Women doctors. Should be an all-male profession.'

'I want to be a doctor,' said a small indignant voice, 'and
m a woman.'

'This is my ally,' Delyth said smugly, hugging Ruth.

'I am truly sorry,' he said. 'I apologise to both you
dies.'

he evening meal was an occasion, and a very enjoyable
ne. They all—including Ruth—sat at the great oak table.
he lady walker, Marie Brown, had returned. She was in
er fifties, a collector of wild flowers. James sat opposite
elyth. Somehow Ruth had managed to sit next to her and
arie was on the other side.

After a few minutes' casual conversation Delyth discov-

ered that Marie was more than a collector of wild flowers–
she was an expert on the therapeutic use of herbs. They ha
a fascinating conversation. 'Did you know that some cour
try folk knew about penicillin years before it was discov
ered?' Marie asked. 'Not as such, of course, but they kne
that putting some moulds on wounds might cure them.'

The meal was wonderful. There were carafes of the loc
wine on the table. After a cold vichyssoise they had por
casseroled in prunes, with a few simply steamed vegetable
Apparently the region was famous for prunes, and Delyt
determined to take some back. Dessert was a tradition:
French *crème caramel*. The food was served slowly, an ac
knowledgment that conversation was as important as food

After the meal Ruth was taken to bed, and with the coffe
Tom gave everyone a tiny brandy. Delyth was about to r
fuse, but James said she should take it. It was like liqui
gold, again a local brand. 'I must take some of this back
she said, 'for my family and for a doctor who's helped m
a lot. James, are you going to take some back for anyone'

She didn't quite understand his answer. 'Yes,' he sai
thoughtfully. 'I'll take a couple of bottles back for a youn
doctor I quite admire.'

It had been a wonderful day, but at the end of the me:
James saw that Delyth was tired. 'I'm feeling the strain, to
a bit,' he said. 'I think we both need to sleep. I'll come bac
early tomorrow again and if you like we'll do a little loc:
tour. Perhaps a walk by the river or a couple of villages?

Her heart caught. 'I'd love that,' she said.

Yesterday had been wonderful, but today was one of thos
magic times. Delyth knew that inconsequential memorie
were often the strongest. She remembered that time she ha
read about what was needed to become a doctor and ha
realised, I could do this. She remembered earlier, whe
she'd been a tiny bridesmaid for her sister Bethany, and ha

been firmly convinced that all that ceremony had been for her. She remembered being an anxious teenager, helping her doctor friend Alun Roberts, and an old lady patient had said, 'You've got lovely gentle hands, dear.'

Today was different. Perhaps James wouldn't remember—but she would.

He picked her up just after lunch. Said they wouldn't drive too far—there was no need to. First they walked along the sandy shore of a fast flowing river, then they drove up to a village perched on the crest of a hill. They walked along the rampart, inspected the church, smiled at the village priest. Then they went to a café and sat on the terrace. It overlooked the village square, and in front of them was a fountain. Somehow the splashing sound made the afternoon even more complete.

She looked at the old stone buildings, felt the warmth of the sun on her face, smelt the southern sun never experienced in England. James ordered himself an iced beer, and for her an odd French herbal drink, slightly alcoholic and very refreshing.

She knew she looked well. Her yellow sundress showed as much of her as she thought proper. Her hair flowed in a great train down her back, secured only by a scrunchie. Ruth had brushed her hair industriously after she had shampooed it.

He looked good too, wearing brown twill trousers, brown sandals and a plain white T-shirt. A simple cheap outfit, and in it he looked gorgeous.

'You look pensive,' he said. 'Tell me what you're thinking.'

Perhaps she was still ill and it stopped her from thinking of the consequences of her reply. Perhaps it was the sheer wonder of the day. After all, it was the kind of question that

demanded a flippant answer. She didn't give one. She was
completely honest.

'I was thinking,' she said, 'that if I am never happier than
I am now, I will be content with my life.'

When she looked at him she realised he recognised how
much she had felt that reply. He reached over the table
stroked her hand.

'I presume part of your happiness is being with me?'

She didn't speak, merely nodded.

'You know that that is the kind of remark that demands
a serious answer. Delyth, at the moment I don't think I can
give it.'

'You could try,' she suggested tentatively.

He paused, a long, long pause. 'You know that means
making comparisons with what I felt for Erin and for
Hilary,' he said, and instantly she was horrified.

'James, I didn't think. I'm sorry. I didn't mean to…'

He leaned over to kiss her, a light butterfly kiss but on
the lips. 'Delyth, the past must be part of the present, but it
doesn't overwhelm it. You're good for me.' His voice hard-
ened. 'Since…since I thought I had found happiness with
one woman, and then another…and then lost both, I decided
happiness for me wasn't with a mate. I've told you, I look
for friends, casual love affairs, satisfaction in my work. I
don't know if I can, if I could…'

It was her turn to kiss him on the lips. They were salty
but sweet. 'Hush,' she said, 'this is a lovely drink, a gorgeous afternoon, wonderful surroundings. I'm with you and
I'm happy. I think you feel the same. I'm sorry I started us
both thinking. Let's just be and enjoy. And you can start by
kissing me again.'

'All right,' he said, and did. The surprising thing was, she
knew she was right. The afternoon was as happy as it had
been before. And she knew he was happy too.

They drove to another hilltop village and walked hand in

and through it. Down a side street was a curio shop, given
alf to tourist attractions, half to junk. They went in to
rowse, there was nothing much that interested them. Then
e picked up something from the floor, and said, 'I'll buy
his for Megan.'

She looked at it—a piece of cast iron with a face on it,
alf ugly, half disturbing. 'Megan would like that,' Delyth
aid, 'though I don't. You know my sister's tastes, don't
ou? But why buy her something?'

'Because I like her a lot.'

'I told you she warned me against you. Said she couldn't
ead your face.'

'She did that out of love for you. That makes me like her
ne more.'

She watched as he paid for the piece and had it wrapped.
'hen they walked to another set of ramparts, and read an
ccount of how the village was once fortified, had been
ttacked and had repelled a small army, though with great
oss of life. Now the landscape in front of them was beau-
ful, serene.

He said, 'Once real people like you and me stood here,
aw enemies coming to attack their village. How d'you
hink they felt?'

It was an interesting question. 'Frightened, of course,' she
aid. 'And perhaps…it made them think more honestly
bout things.'

They paced on further, both, she thought, quite happy.
'hen, abruptly, she asked, 'I want your medical opinion. I
ad an injury to my head. Am I completely recovered?'

'My medical opinion?' His voice was surprised.

'Imagine I've come into one of your clinics. You've got
ny case notes. Am I completely recovered?'

'Not quite. Physically you're a bit below par. Your wrist
as been redressed, it's a bit stiff but you can use it.
Mentally you're perfectly competent.'

'Thank you, Doctor, I agree with your diagnosis. I asked you, by the way, for your sake not mine. Remember when we nearly made love, and you turned me down, partly because I was a virgin?'

His answer was hoarse. 'You brought this up, Delyth. I would never have done so. Yes, I remember. It was one of the hardest things I've ever done in my life.'

'Good,' she said complacently. 'I'm looking forward to tonight's meal. I enjoyed last night and I'll go to bed early again. Your room is next to mine. I'm going to come to it when everyone is in bed. This is my decision, what I want. You haven't pressured me in any way at all.' She looked at him curiously. 'You do want me, don't you?'

His face was half stricken, half elated. 'Want you! Delyth, I—'

'Well, you can always lock your door.'

By mutual assent they stopped and gazed across the fertile green valley. Then she took her hand out of her pocket and showed him three silver foil packets. 'I bought these on the boat,' she said. 'They're for us. I'm not getting pregnant while I'm still training. Take them.'

They stood like two stone statues for a moment. 'Why have you changed your mind?' he asked.

'When I was locked in that cellar I thought I might be killed. I thought about all the decisions I'd made, all the things I hadn't done. And being with you was one of them. I've thought about it quite a lot since. Now I know what I want.' She nodded at her still outstretched hand. 'Are you going to take these?'

Then he reached out. 'I'll take them,' he said.

They drove back to Les Cabines. A mile before they arrived she put her hand on his arm. 'Can we stop here a minute?' she asked.

He pulled onto the grass verge and looked at her questioningly. She kissed him quickly. 'I want you to know that

oved what we nearly did last time,' she said, 'and I want
night to be as good. I'm coming to your bedroom and I
ly ask one thing—that you say you want me to.'

'Oh, how I do,' he muttered, pulling her to him. 'Delyth,
lo. But I'll come to your—'

'No. This is my decision. I'll come to you.'

Perhaps because the night had been sorted out in her
ind, she enjoyed the evening. What was to come had been
cided. There was another magnificent meal, but with dif-
rent people to talk to. She sat between Alan and nearly
aude. It was nearly Claude because somehow Ruth had
anaged to insert herself next to Delyth again. She didn't
y much, was quite happy to listen. Delyth liked her.

After the meal Ruth went to bed and they played silly but
joyable word games. Then they all went to bed. Her heart
ating, she changed into her nightie and sat in the darkness
aiting till the bumps and footsteps outside were silent. She
aited another ten minutes. Then she padded into the hall
d tried James's door. It was open. She slipped inside the
rk room.

Their two rooms were at one end of the barn—there was
chance of them being overheard. Like her, he had French
ndows at the far end of his room, and had drawn the
rtains back. By starlight she could see him sitting on the
d. He was mostly shadow, but there was the gleam of arm
d thigh. He was naked, and it seemed entirely proper.

She pushed down the shoulder straps of her nightie,
aited till it fell in a soft pile at her feet, then stepped
rward. Now she, too, was naked. 'I've been waiting for
is,' she told him. He stood to fold her to him, the feel of
r skin against his exquisite. But as yet he didn't hold her
htly.

'Delyth, are you sure you want us to…? I mean, nothing
s changed and I…'

So she pressed forward and leaned against him, feeling

her breasts against the muscles of his chest. 'Stop talking,' she ordered. 'I know what I want…what we want.'

Her words were all he needed. His mouth found hers, and now he pulled her to him. She felt her nipples grow proud as they rubbed against the fine hair. For a moment they stood crushed together, then he relaxed. 'No hurry, no hurry,' he whispered. 'We have all the time in the world.'

He eased her down onto the bed beside him. With a small sigh of comic relief she realised that his bed was also double. She lay there, content to wait and to wonder.

'You're beautiful,' he murmured, 'so beautiful.' His hand stroked her, just the softest touch of fingertips, from her chin, across her breasts, the gentle rise of her stomach to the warm places below. The breath caught in her throat at that, and he heard her alarm. 'Don't worry,' he reassured her, 'we have time, so much time.'

So she lay there as he continued his gentle caresses, feeling her body relax under his hands. She was afloat in a sea of sensation, her entire world nothing but the warmth, the comfort of his touching. I could lie here for ever, she thought.

After a while she wondered if she was being selfish. Tentatively, she put out a hand to stroke his neck, the rounded shoulders. Her fingers grazed his nipples and he sighed. He likes that as much as I do, she thought. Greatly daring, she moved her hand downwards and he groaned as she clasped his erect manhood.

'I didn't hurt you, did I?' she asked, alarmed.

His voice was thick, but amused. 'No, you didn't hurt me, Delyth. In fact, quite the opposite.'

Now he leaned over to kiss her. Instinctively, she knew what to do. She wrapped her arms around him, pulled him over her. First there was the delicious weight of his body on hers. Then, when she was quite ready, she opened herself to him. 'My love, my love,' he panted, and there was the

efest moment of discomfort for her. It didn't last long.
was gentle with her and soon she found herself moving
th him with a rhythm that was automatic, and easy to
low. She felt the impetus of him growing, her own body
ithed beneath his, and then suddenly, like a shock for both
them, they came together in a climax that had her moan-
g in delirious joy. 'My darling,' he muttered.

She didn't care, she stayed with him through the night. It
is so good to feel his sleeping body next to hers, feel the
elling of his chest as he breathed, the warmth of his
eath. He lay on his back and she on her side, one arm and
e leg across him, only a sheet covering them. When he
ned, his arm slid round her automatically, and she loved

They woke early, and he made love to her again. After-
rds they lay together, happy in each other's arms. There
is an hour before they needed to rise, but neither wanted
sleep.

'Are we going to do this again?' he asked.

'Don't think I'm going to let you go now,' she answered.
'e'll do it every night while we're here, and then when
're back in London.'

She felt his body stiffen with unease. 'I may not be in
ndon for ever,' he pointed out.

Quickly she kissed him. 'I know what you're thinking.
u're going to say that I must remember that, although
u're very fond of me, this is only an interlude. I must
member that you travel light. There's a chance you might
offered a job in America. If you are you'll take it and
ve me behind. Isn't that true?'

He winced. 'I wouldn't have put it quite as baldly as that
t, yes, I was thinking something like that.'

'Don't worry. I know that's what you're thinking.' Her
ice was quite calm.

He sat up, looked down at her face on the pillow, pulled

gently at the long hair that flowed over her shoulders. 'A
you're quite happy with that?'

She had to get this right. 'I should be sorry to see y
go, but even sorrier if you felt guilty about it.'

He was still obviously uneasy. 'Delyth, I don't want y
to think... I don't want you to delude yourself and ta
advantage of that.'

She also sat up, and hugged him. 'Listen,' she said che
fully, 'I'll spell it out for you. If you want to go to Ameri
then I'll be very happy for you to go. And if you want
stay with me, then I'll be equally happy. Does that set yc
mind at rest?'

'After a fashion,' he said, looking puzzled. 'Because
know that you mean it. But I don't understand it.'

'You don't need to.' She glanced at his bedside cloc
'Come on, time to get up. You can go first in the bathroc
and I'll sneak back next door.'

He dragged on his robe, stole one last kiss and went o

She lay back in bed, her arms behind her head, a cc
tented smile on her face. Who knew what the future wo
bring? But it was better to have James Owen for a wh
than never at all.

He decided not to go into hospital until later. Instead
showering, he fetched his kit from the car, changed into
and shouted to Delyth through the bedroom door that
was going for a run.

'Why the sudden change of plan?' he heard her surpris
voice ask, but he didn't answer. He wasn't quite sure.

There was comfort in the accustomed exercise. As usu
he stretched first, then set off up the narrow country lane
his usual easy starting pace. To each side of him the fie
and woods of Aquitaine stretched out, scenes which n
mally would have entranced him. Not today.

He was warm now, and he increased his pace. The sl

of his feet on the gravel grew faster. There was exhilaration in the physical pain—in the gasping of his lungs, the acid burn in his calves and thighs. For a while he held it, then slowed to a speed that was fast but endurable. Now he could think. What should he do about Delyth?

There had been two terrible episodes in his life, and after them he had sworn to himself that never again would he put his happiness solely in the hands of one woman. He wouldn't risk that kind of pain again. And his life had been fulfilled enough. There had been gentle love affairs, in which neither party gave or expected too much.

But now Delyth was giving him so much. He knew already that he couldn't just walk out of her life. She was becoming necessary to him. He...he *loved* her. It was the first time he had acknowledged the fact. Bitterly he made himself say it out loud. 'I love her.'

Now what? He couldn't just overturn the way of life, the mind-set that had kept him reasonably happy for the past six years. He knew that Delyth was deceiving herself. She didn't want a temporary love affair. Ultimately she needed—she deserved—a full commitment. Could he—did he want—to give it?

There was no answer. He sprinted again, looking to the physical pain to hide his mental turmoil.

CHAPTER TEN

DELYTH accepted James going for a run without question. They had breakfast together, she waved him off to work then wiped the sweat from her forehead.

'It's going to be hot and it's going to be sticky,' Val told her. 'Shall I make some iced fruit juice?'

Delyth told her that would be lovely. She looked at the sky—dirty grey-yellow clouds covered yesterday's sun, but it was much, much hotter. She was glad she could sit here in shorts and light shirt.

The fruit juice was refreshing, but any cooling effect was temporary. Soon she was hot again, and the box of tissues she fetched quickly emptied as she wiped her brow again and again. There was no sitting in the shade—the heat was all-invasive.

She had to think. There was a chair facing the fields and then the long line of hills. She'd sit there and hope the peace of the landscape would calm her fretful imaginings.

She'd meant what she'd said to James. He could go to America if he wanted, but she hoped that ultimately he wouldn't want to. She loved him. Because she loved him she had invited him to her bed—that was what lovers did. If they did part then she would have had something of him.

Lord, it was hot. She felt lethargic but restless at the same time. She fetched her book and more juice, but couldn't settle to doing anything. Ruth came to talk to her and say goodbye for a few days. She was going to stay with friends in one of the valleys.

'We'll all feel better when it rains,' she told Delyth. 'It doesn't stay like this for too long.'

'I'm glad. Where are you going?'

'I'm going to St Martin—it's a lovely village. Lots of places to explore.'

Val joined them, agreeing with her daughter. 'She's in and out of everyone's house,' she told Delyth. 'It's the way they are there.'

Delyth just couldn't face lunch. She waved goodbye to Val and Tom as they drove off with Ruth, then just sat waiting. She swam for a while, but had less energy than usual, and when she climbed out of the pool the air seemed thicker than ever.

She sat, trying to read. After a while a flash in the distance caught her eye. She looked up to see lightning playing round the hills in the distance. There were sheets of it, flickering like nothing she'd ever seen in England. It was beautiful to watch. Then, for the first time all day, a cool breeze came up.

Alan and Claude returned early. 'We just couldn't work,' Alan said. 'It was too sticky and we've been here before—we know what's coming.'

'This is Aquitaine, the watery place,' said Claude. 'Would you like a coffee?'

To her surprise she found that she would. 'You'd better come under the verandah too,' said Alan. 'Won't be long now.'

It started to rain. First there were just occasional heavy drops, landing on the paving stones with a loud splat. Another stronger and cooler breeze rose, then the rattling drops turned into the downpour proper. Now she felt comfortable, better than she had all day. With the others she sat under the verandah, sipping coffee, exhilarated, watching the rain.

She had been in storms like this in England, but usually after a few minutes it either stopped or slowed. Here the rain was relentless. After a while she felt subdued by the sheer power of it. 'Good thing Les Cabines is on a hill,' Alan said. 'There'll be flooding in the valleys.'

Delyth was glad to see James come home—he'd phoned to say he'd be late. She watched him pull his coat over his head and sprint the few yards to the verandah. 'Lots of road accidents today,' he told her. 'This rain after the heat of the past few days makes the roads very treacherous. I've done a couple of abdominals and a crushed chest this afternoon.'

She followed him to his room and watched as he pulled off his damp clothes. Then she hugged him. 'I'm looking forward to being in bed with you,' she told him. 'And I know we're in France but I don't want to feel as if I'm taking part in an old-fashioned French farce. It's silly, hopping between bedrooms like a couple of teenagers. I want to move in with you.'

'It's your reputation,' he said with a grin. 'You know there's nothing I want more.'

'I'll fetch my cases now.'

They joined the others on the verandah—people enjoyed looking at the rain. When asked, James described the operations he had performed that afternoon. 'The chest had been crushed by the steering-wheel—it's a very common condition. If they'd seen what I see, more people would wear their safety belts! Anyway, I cut through the ribs on the left side and found...'

His audience was enthralled. Delyth had forgotten how fascinated people could be by medicine.

Afterwards she told him, 'I'm starting to miss work now, I think I've nearly recovered. Could I come into the hospital with you, have a look round, perhaps do a bit? After all, I am a doctor.'

He laughed. 'Rest for another day, but after that I see no reason why not. Take it easy at first.'

They had another enjoyable evening meal. Tom prowled

around upstairs, looking for leaks, and was pleased when there were none. James wanted to be in hospital very promptly the next day so they went to bed extra early. Their love-making was as joyful as ever. Throughout the night she kept waking, happy in his arms, and listened to the rain thudding down outside, as implacable as ever.

By lunchtime the next day it still hadn't stopped, and she was beginning to feel depressed. Val came over and said the forecast wasn't at all good—the rain looked like lasting for some days to come. 'It can really rain hard here,' she said, looking worried, 'and it's exceptionally bad about every five or six years. This might be that time. They've done a lot of flood control work recently so things should be all right. But you never know. This isn't what you want for your convalescence.'

In the afternoon she accepted a lift from Alan and Claude, and they drove down to the nearest big village. They ran through the rain to admire the church, and then went to a museum of country life. Alan pointed out old photographs of the village, just recognisable under three feet of water, with boats being rowed up the main street.

'I hope all this flood control works,' he said.

They rushed back to the car and drove over a bridge that crossed a stream, a tributary of the main river. She remembered it when they first came, a pleasant little brook. Now it was grey and greasy, well up the banks and running fast. She shivered. This was an odd country, too many extremes. In Wales, you usually knew what to expect.

When they returned to Les Cabines Val told her that James had phoned. Today he'd be back very late—there had been a lot of emergencies. She sat with the others for the evening meal but didn't eat much. She wanted to eat with James when he arrived. The constant rainfall was now depressing the others. It was noticeable that there wasn't the same cheerfulness as the previous night.

He didn't get in until past ten. She didn't mind—no one knew better than she what medical emergencies were like. He was obviously tired when he arrived so she fetched him a meal, having told Val that she'd look after him.

'I'm earning my keep,' he told her. 'I've been operating most of the day, cases that would normally be shipped to Toulon. But they're under pressure too. How fit d'you feel?'

'I'm fit enough for work,' she told him, 'and my French is just good enough to get by.'

He shook his head. 'I want you to assist me in Theatre. That will free a French doctor. But I think you're not quite fully fit yet so you're only to work a moderate day.'

'Fine, I promise,' she said. 'But won't there be problems with insurance or something?'

'This is an emergency. The French are great at cutting red tape when they want to. There'll be no trouble with you working.'

The theatre at the Villeneuf hospital wasn't quite as well equipped as those in her own hospital, Delyth discovered next day, but she was surprised at how easily she slipped into the regime. The instruments were the same—she recognised the names of many of the manufacturers. Quickly she realised that many of the technical terms were the same. The only different thing was that the coffee was of a much higher quality. Many of the staff spoke to her in English, and most of the doctors there seemed to have some knowledge of it. She felt at home.

It was good to watch James operate again. In spite of her strapped-up wrist she was able to assist, and she knew she was a real help to him. In the morning they had a man with a case of pyloric stenosis, the muscular exit of the stomach had narrowed because of an ulcer nearby. It was a satisfying operation, she knew that afterwards the man's condition would improve considerably. He had been losing weight becoming dehydrated.

Later on they performed a gastrectomy, removing part of the stomach of a man who had an ulcer that just would not heal. 'There may be some unpleasant post-gastrectomy syndromes,' he told her, 'but this operation was certainly necessary.'

At five in the afternoon James said, 'Don't argue. You've finished for the day. I've arranged with Tom to pick you up out at the front.'

'But there's more to do,' Delyth protested. 'I'm fine. I want to stay.'

'You can come again tomorrow. You know you've been a considerable help today, but I won't have you overtired.'

She felt like rebelling. But he wasn't an easy man to cross, and she knew he could be right. 'I'll be back when I can,' he told her. 'You know I'm looking forward to it.'

'OK, I'll go, then. But don't think this gives you a licence to boss me about.' She smiled to show she didn't really mean it.

He came into the barn later than ever, and she could tell he was exhausted. She fed him, then sent him straight to bed. 'I'll be with you in a minute,' she told him, 'and no sex tonight—you're far too tired. Just a hug and a promise.'

He managed to smile. 'I'm not too worried about the work,' he told her. 'In Africa I had a couple of emergencies like this. The French seem on top of things. Did you know that in France all emergencies are dealt with first by *sapeurs-pompiers*, the fire brigade? They're trained paramedics.'

She hadn't known that. It seemed an interesting idea.

Next day she helped James again in Theatre. They weren't quite so busy. Most of the time they dealt with the results of road accidents, repairing crushed and cut bodies. In the afternoon a cheery French orthopaedic surgeon came in to work with them. There was a particularly nasty crush injury to a woman's pelvis, and he reconstructed the bones while James tried to deal with torn muscles and veins. It was delicate work, and he performed it at speed.

Inside the operating theatre they were screened from the outside world, but when they came out they were again aware of the non-stop rain. They got back reasonably early. Val told them that the news was bad—there had been considerable flooding and it was thought there'd be no let-up in the rain. Things were getting serious, and the government had moved a unit of soldiers nearby.

Because of everyone's low spirits, Val had made a special effort with the evening meal. She'd cooked a duck and mushroom pie, with a blissfully light crust. There was a special effort made by everyone to cheer up. Delyth herself wasn't depressed, just the opposite. She felt she was getting stronger and ready to get back to work. Apart from that, she had James.

He sat by her at the great table, now candle-lit, drinking red wine. She leaned against him. Casually he would stroke her side and brush the long hair from her face. At night she always let her hair down—she knew he loved it.

He'd been attacking superstition again, and surprisingly had found a worthy opponent in Marie Brown. The older lady claimed there was a lot of truth in folk stories. Some so-called superstitions were quite reasonable beliefs. 'Willow was known as a painkiller long before aspirin,' she pointed out. 'Cobwebs *are* good for wounds if you've got nothing better to put on. And what about acupuncture? Even fifteen years ago it was regarded as the province of charlatans. Now many GPs practise it. It's accepted by the BMA.'

Delyth had to smile at the vehemence of the old lady and the grace with which James accepted the force of her argument. 'You're entirely right on all of the points,' he said.

It was a more pleasant evening than they'd had for

while. 'Still an evil night,' Tom said. 'I think we'll have a special treat. I'll fetch the brandy from the house.'

He came rushing back. 'Just caught the telephone,' he gasped. 'James, will you come and take it? An emergency— sounds a really bad one.'

The two men ran out. No one round the table spoke, waiting for what was to come. Then James returned, his face set.

'Big trouble,' he said. 'They need all the doctors and nurses they can round up. They know I've had some experience in disaster management.'

He turned to Delyth, not as a lover but as a coldly assessing doctor. 'You've been ill. Are you fit enough to work all night, perhaps outside in rough conditions? Give me an honest answer—this isn't a test. You'll be worse than useless if you collapse or something.'

'I'm fit enough,' she answered frostily. 'I'm not a man, letting testosterone talk for me.'

He gave her a grim smile. 'That's what I thought. Get dressed in rough clothes, boots and anorak. Bring a complete change in a bag—you might get wet through. And put your hair up. We'll be picked up in five minutes.'

The others clustered round him, asking for details, but he didn't seem to know much. When she had changed they all went outside onto the verandah. It was dark, still raining. In the valley they saw the smudged lights of a vehicle coming towards them.

Eventually it splashed into the courtyard. It was a large van with great wheels. On the sides were fastened spades, drums, a ladder, tools that might be needed in a rescue. With James she jumped into a cramped little space, already nearly filled by men in canvas overalls and helmets. Then James was deep in conversation in French with the senior man there. There wasn't much chance for her to attend. She had to hang on grimly as they bumped and rolled onwards. The driver wanted to get somewhere in a hurry. And the rain pelted down.

They drove for perhaps three quarters of an hour. Towards the end she knew they were climbing, presumably a narrow road—she could tell by the straining engine, the difficulty in getting round corners. There was the odd glimpse of overhanging trees, steep banks. Finally they stopped. The man in charge snapped out a series of curt orders. The others seemed to know instantly what to do. Delyth followed James, her hood up against the rain.

They stepped out and heard the rattle of generators, saw great arclights among the trees, a huddle of vehicles. There were two great tents so they ran towards them.

'All this has been set up in the past two hours,' James said. 'I'm very impressed. This is the first staging post. There will be relays of ambulances, taking people down to hospital. We'll also take the young and the old. Lots of people won't need hospital attention, but they'll be cold, wet, miserable and perhaps shocked. We've to get them warm, get food in them, reassure them and find them somewhere to sleep. Then they'll survive. People can die in situations like this, not because they're seriously injured but because they've not been looked after.'

He pointed to one of the tents. 'There are campbeds in there, blankets, a mobile kitchen. But we triage everyone in this tent. You might be acting as a doctor, but you're more likely to be needed as a nurse and auxiliary. That OK?'

'Fine by me. I'll do what's necessary.' She was excited to be working with him again. 'But, James, what exactly has happened? I don't know.'

'Sorry! It's all happened so fast. There's a village in a valley just below us. Above it were two dams, old ones. The lower dam broke its banks because the upper one was over-full. The water was funnelled down the valley, and a wall of it smashed through the village. Many of the houses were knocked down and some people are trapped. Everyone is being evacuated. We've got army engineers looking at the top dam—they think that might go too. It's bigger, and if it breaks what's left of the village will be just flattened.'

Somehow, she knew. 'James, what's the village called?' she asked.

He frowned. 'St Martin.'

'That's the village Ruth is staying in with friends. She's here somewhere. James, we have to find her!'

There was no place for personal feelings in disaster management. Neither James nor Delyth could look—that was the job of another team. James promised he would make enquiries but she knew that her anguish would have to be contained. She was a doctor with a job to do! She was taken into the larger tent and introduced to a doctor who fortunately spoke excellent English. 'My name is Etienne,' he told her. 'Later perhaps we may become acquainted. Please help me with these new arrivals.'

She was impressed by the efficiency. Although it was a tent, they were on a hard floor, there were examination couches behind screens and trolleys with instruments. She was found a white coat.

As Etienne spoke a group of wet, mudstained people were ushered in. Orderlies separated them into male and female, helped them out of wet clothes, gave them blankets and offered hot drinks. Delyth noticed an old lady who seemed bewildered by what was going on. She would be her first patient.

With a nurse, she helped the old lady undress, then conducted a quick examination. It wasn't a good sign that the lady neither commented nor objected, but limply let them do what they liked with her. She had been wet through, but although it wasn't too cold it had been sufficient to produce hypothermia. Delyth guessed that her patient's core temperature was below 30 degrees. But she wasn't shivering.

The nurse quickly recognised what was wrong. After wrapping the old lady in blankets, she rushed to fetch a silver space blanket to wrap around them. The old lady's body temperature should now slowly come back to normal. It was important not to warm her too quickly. The nurse now seemed happy. Delyth was not. Something was wrong. Summoning what little French she had, she said, *'Diabétique?'*

The nurse looked at her curiously, and then realisation struck. She went to question the other people who had come in. There was a flurry of French, and the nurse returned to say, *'Oui, diabétique. Pardon, madame.'* She shouted something and a moment later the old lady was swept away on her stretcher. Recovering from hypothermia when diabetic, that was much more tricky. She would need careful management.

Nothing much else was exciting, though she was kept busy. There were cuts that needed cleaning and a couple that needed careful dressing. She also irrigated the eyes of a sobbing woman who had fallen in the mud with her eyes open. Delyth carefully rolled back the upper and lower lids, then, using her ophthalmoscope, she looked for signs of scratching or injury. There were none. The woman, now much quieter, was given soothing drops.

There was a lull, then in came a young soldier, a field dressing pressed to his forearm. Delyth lifted it to look—a nasty deep cut made by something sharp. She and the nurse cleaned the cut, then Delyth sutured it. The soldier stared stonily ahead. When she had finished Delyth called for Etienne, who, she could see, wasn't busy.

'I think this boy should rest for a couple of hours before he starts work again,' she said.

'I agree entirely.' Etienne spoke rapidly to the boy, but

she couldn't follow what was being said—only that the young soldier was agreeing. Then the nurse put on a thick dressing, and the soldier walked to the tent door. But, instead of turning to the rest tent as he had been directed, he turned the other way.

Etienne shrugged. 'I could report him to his senior officer for disobeying orders,' he said, and winked at her.

A smiling man came round with a great mug of coffee. It smelt wonderful. Looking at her watch, Delyth saw that she had been working for four hours. Time was passing. She forced herself not to think of Ruth. James had said he would make what enquiries he could—she would just have to wait and hope. She had noticed one or two cases carried by stretcher straight into a curtained-off area. They were the dead. She shivered.

There were fewer cases now. She had time to chat to her nurse, whose name was Monique, even sit in a chair. She went to peer into the section of the tent where the more serious cases were being dealt with. They, too, seemed to be working less frantically. Etienne smiled and waved. She looked outside. It was still raining. It seemed less dark; dawn was breaking.

Then James came out of the darkness towards her. He was dressed in overalls, like the others, and wearing high boots and a helmet. He was covered in mud, and his face looked more tired than she'd ever seen it before. He looked defeated. She felt a great rush of love for him. She herself was dog-tired. She wondered how long it would be before he could shower, and they could tumble together into his double bed. But there were other questions first. 'Ruth?' she asked, and agony lanced through her when he shook his head. 'She's missing.'

Etienne had also come to the tent door. After another swift exchange James said, 'There's not so much work for you here now. I want you to come with me. There's a

job…just for you.' She thought he sounded uncomfortable
But Etienne shook her by the hand, thanked her and said h
hoped they would meet again soon in happier circumstances
Monique kissed her. Then James was walking her quickl
towards a waiting Jeep.

'Tell me about Ruth,' she said. 'What does ''missing'
mean? Is she…is she likely to be dead?'

They climbed into the Jeep, and it eased forward. 'In
situation like this,' James said, 'one of the first jobs is t
ask everybody where they were, and who they were wit
when the water hit. That way we can cross-check that every
body has been found. In fact, we fetched two old ladies ot
of a bedroom a couple of hours ago. They'd slept throug
everything. But Ruth had gone out to visit friends. Sh
didn't say which ones—she was friendly with everyone–
so we don't know where to look. She's the only one ur
accounted for.'

In spite of the rain it was getting lighter now, and Delyt
could distinguish trees alongside them. 'Where are we gc
ing?' she asked.

'We're going to the village of St Martin.'

The road was precipitously steep, and she winced as sh
thought of the drivers who must have negotiated these ev
bends. Then the Jeep stopped where a few other vehicle
were parked. James and Delyth climbed out. They went t
the edge of a cliff and below them was the village of S
Martin.

Through its centre raced a stream, obviously usually sma
but now the size of a small river, carrying debris includin
small trees. She could see where the flood had hit—builc
ings had been knocked down and those houses still standin
had their ground-floor doors and windows knocked ou
There were groups of men searching.

'The whole village will have to be rebuilt,' said Jame
'perhaps in a more sensible spot than below two old dams

e led her to the largest vehicle and they looked into what
as obviously a command post. There was a radio, sheets
papers, supplies.

James talked rapidly to the man in charge. The man
oked worried, shook his head, tapped his watch. He
anced at Delyth. 'Fifteen minutes,' he said. 'Fifteen
inutes *justement.*'

Delyth looked at the whiteness round James's eyes, saw
e channels of pink skin where sweat had trickled through
ud and dirt. Her heart went out to him, he looked so des-
rate. He took her by the arm, and when he spoke she
uld tell he was near collapse. 'The army engineers say
e top dam will go at any time. It will certainly flatten
ything that's left. In fifteen minutes he's ordering his men
ck up here. Very properly, he won't risk their lives.'

He grabbed her other arm and pulled her round to face
m. 'Ruth is the only one left unaccounted for. Perhaps
e's already dead. But something tells me she's still alive
d still in the village. She's trapped, and she's going to be
lled.'

'Something tells you?' she asked flatly.

'Something tells me. I can't get it out of my head. I want
u to come down there with me, see if this…power you've
t can find her. The men just don't have time to search
erywhere. And it's too wet for the dogs.'

She stood still in the rain, looking at him in horror. It
as the last thing she had expected.

'It just happens,' she said. 'I can't turn it on—it just hap-
ns. Sometimes not for months.'

His shoulders sagged. 'Of course,' he said. 'Silly of me
ask. Will you wait for me in the car? I'll be with you
on.'

'No. I'll come down and do what I can. But don't…don't
ly on me.'

They slithered down to the village main street and waded

cautiously over the bridge which had not yet been swe
away. He walked just behind her but didn't speak or tou
her, except to steady her when she stumbled. She walked
the top of the village main—and almost only—street, turn
and looked downwards.

She didn't know what to do. On her left was what h
once been the Café des Sports. Now its windows we
smashed, the pillars at the front bent. Water had rag
through the single room, tumbling chairs and tables toget
against the far wall, and above them there was still a ca
endar advertising Pernod. She shivered, but forced hers
to walk over and step inside the room.

Forget her fatigue, forget her discomfort, forget the nois
around her—the shouts of the searchers, the roar of the riv
the rattle of water dripping on the floor, the creaking a
groaning of the building. Where was Ruth? She tried
empty her mind, to think as—'Delyth, move!' It was h
own name being shouted in that agonised way. She hea
the bang of James's feet on the floor, felt his arm round h
waist and was half thrown, half carried out of the wreck
building. Together they fell, sprawled in the mud outsi
the café.

There was the shriek of bending wood, then a series
sodden thumps. She twisted to look behind her. The fro
of the café had collapsed. Where she had been standing
giant beam had smashed through the floor.

James's face was only inches from hers. Even throu
the mud she could see that it was stricken, ashen-whi
'Delyth, you could have been killed,' he muttered. 'Y
could have been killed. What would I have…?'

Adrenaline flushed through her system—she wasn't tir
any more. She knew it was the fight-or-flight syndrome.
about half an hour her body would react and she'd fe
worse than ever. But not yet. She scrambled to her feet.

'We've got work to do,' she snapped. 'We've got to find Ruth.'

She watched as he fought to gain control over his feelings, to put behind him the horror of what had just nearly happened. He stretched out his arms, flexed the muscles of his neck, clenched his fingers into fists then relaxed them. 'Yes, we've got to find Ruth,' he said, in a voice she barely recognised. 'Delyth, you've got to find Ruth.'

She turned and walked down the main street. She had never tried to turn on this power, didn't know how. Instead she thought of herself as a little girl aged nine, obviously bored after days confined because of the rain. What would she do? What would she think? Where would she go? But now she would be cold, frightened, probably wet, perhaps even injured. She hadn't shouted, had she? Or if she had she hadn't been heard.

She tried to empty her mind, to be a little girl, cold, wet, frightened. Cold, wet, frightened. She slipped, gashing her hand on a protruding spike. She didn't notice the pain but stuck the hand in her pocket. She was in a different world. She was a little girl, cold, wet, frightened.

Once or twice she stopped, gazed blankly at a building, then moved on. Behind her James walked, not allowing himself to think or hope. Then she stopped and rocked on her feet. He put out a hand to steady her, then withdrew it. She pointed. 'There,' she said.

She pointed to an ancient building on the bank of the river, now half under water. Once it had been a washplace for the entire village. Now it was long since abandoned. But behind it was a storeroom, with a door no more than four feet high. The side had been collapsed by the river.

James turned and shouted, and a four-man team ran towards them. Delyth watched wide-eyed as they seemed to take an awfully long time carefully prising open the door. Quite often the act of opening a door makes more of the

building fall down,' James told her. 'You might know tha
now. But these men are well trained.' He slipped his arn
around her shoulders.

The door opened a little. One man peered round it an
shone a torch. Delyth heard him shout. James's grip on he
tightened and she found she had to make herself breathe
No, she didn't. She knew that someone was living
breathing, inside that storeroom.

Two men managed to wriggle inside, then there was
long pause. One of the other men was carrying a radio. I
suddenly crackled. He listened and then turned to hold ou
five fingers. Five minutes left.

'All the men are ordered back,' James said tautly. 'Th
dam won't hold out for long.'

One of the men backed out of the storeroom, carryin
with infinite caution a limp form in a pink dress, with bloo
down one arm. From somewhere a collapsible stretcher ap
peared. Ruth's motionless form was laid on it. Delyth stoo
back as James made the swiftest of examinations, stuck
field dressing onto the injured arm, then stood back to le
the others wrap a space blanket around the little figure.

The four set off at a jog trot, the stretcher between them
James and Delyth followed. They saw the other group
moving out, too. She had to lag behind when they reache
the steep climb out of the village. James held her, encour
aged her. They watched the fitter soldiers race ahead t
place Ruth in the waiting ambulance.

The ambulance didn't move before they got there
Instead, James went inside to conduct a more detailed ex
amination. Delyth sat on the steps outside. A kindly soldie
took out a space blanket and wrapped it around her shoul
ders.

'Come in,' James called after a while. She climbed int
the ambulance. Ruth's eyes were open.

'Hello, Delyth,' she said. 'You found me. I knew you would.' The eyes flickered shut and she slept.

'Nothing seriously wrong,' James said, 'but I'll ride in with her. I'll arrange for you to get a lift home. A night in a hospital bed for Ruth and she'll be fine.' Delyth bowed her head and wept.

She woke as the Jeep stopped at Les Cabines. A soldier half carried her to the verandah. Lights were on and a little group of people was waiting. Marie put her arm round Delyth. 'We've all been up all night,' she said. 'Val and Tom heard about Ruth just after you'd left. They heard she'd been found half an hour ago and they've gone to the hospital. Apparently, you found her?'

Delyth shrugged. 'There were a lot of people looking,' she said. She was more tired than she'd ever been in her life before. She couldn't think, couldn't make decisions, couldn't cope.

'I know what you need,' Marie said, and half dragged her through the barn to the bathroom. Delyth let the older woman undress her and ease her into a warm bath, smelling of something aromatic. She accepted a cup of tea with sugar in it. And after a while she felt a little better. Still tired, but she could think.

She managed to get herself out of the bath and pulled on her nightie. 'What about James?' she asked Marie.

'When that young man of yours appears I'll put him in the bath, then into bed with you.'

'Let him undress himself,' Delyth advised, and staggered into James's room. There was so much to think about and she wasn't going to think about any of it. Outside it was still raining. Her eyes shut the minute her head touched the pillow.

In the middle of the night—or possibly the middle of the morning—she felt someone climb into bed with her. She

felt warmth against her back, an arm round her waist. Sh
smiled, and went back to sleep.

Eventually, she woke. Something was different. Sh
squinted at James's bedside clock. Half past one. She mu
have been very tired. What was different? Then it struc
her—the silence. No constant drumming on the window
and the veranda roof. It had stopped raining.

Beside her was James, still fast asleep. He was lying c
his side, his arm above the sheet. She ran her finger fro
his wrist along the muscles of forearm and biceps to h
rounded shoulder and his neck. He slept on. So she kisse
his shoulder, and still he slept. Less sleep than she'd had

Without disturbing him, she wriggled out of bed and p
on her robe. Peering through the window, she saw a wea
sun, the first for days. She walked to the kitchen.

Alan and Claude were there. 'Everyone's asleep,' Ala
explained. 'Last night—this morning—was hard on ever
one. Are you all right now, Delyth?'

'I'm fine now. But last night took it out of me.'

'You can tell us all about it later. Sit there, I'll make yc
a drink. Tea or coffee?'

'Coffee, I think, and make it strong. Can I have tw
mugs?'

She took the coffee on a tray back to the bedroom. Aft
glancing in the mirror, she pulled a comb through her hai
In the night it had come undone. Then she slid in besi
James again. The rich aroma of coffee filled the room, ar
after a while a voice from the pillow said, 'That smel
good. Is there one for me?'

'If you want to sit up.' He did. She looked at his tousle
hair, unshaven face, sleepy expression. 'You look a mess
she said, 'but I love you. Here's an early afternoon kiss.'

'You don't look a mess,' he said in reply. 'You loc

ncredibly beautiful, and here's a kiss back.' His took
onger.

'Drink your coffee,' she said after a while. 'You must
eed it. Er…how's Ruth?'

'She's good. Val and Tom are with her. She's shocked
nd scared, but there's nothing seriously wrong and they'll
robably discharge her tomorrow. She's only alive thanks
o you, Delyth.'

'Coffee, I said! We can be serious later when you've
oken up.'

So they finished their coffee and then he fetched more.
Ie climbed back into bed. 'If we're going to be decadent
e'll do it in style,' he told her. 'We have to talk.'

'Sounds serious again. It was a hard night. I'm not sure
want this right now.'

'I've heard that you can't have everything you want in
is life.' His smile took the sting from his words. 'But I
ink I can. Delyth, I want an honest answer. I told you I
ould only have a temporary affair with you. I tried to be
ir with you. But you came to bed with me anyway. Was
because you thought that I didn't mean it?'

Her reply was reflective. 'I just didn't know, James. But
me time with you, even a little, was better than no time
 all.'

'So it wasn't this feeling, this voice you have, that told
ou to do it?'

'No. And before you scoff, you have that feeling some-
mes too. You knew Ruth was in that village last night,
idn't you?'

'Possibly,' he sighed, 'or possibly I just wanted her to be
ere. Tell me, how did you find her?'

'I just imagined I was a little girl. Where would I hide or
lay? And then it just came to me.'

'So it wasn't something…something paranormal?' His
oice was eager.

'Yes, James, I think it was,' she said gently. 'And y[o]
think the same.'

'Perhaps.' He was silent a moment, his face sudden[ly]
sombre. 'Too much happened yesterday, Delyth. I'm st[ill]
trying to get it in order in my mind. D'you realise you we[re]
nearly killed?'

She had forgotten! 'I suppose I have to thank you,' s[he]
said slowly. 'You pulled me out of that café just in tim[e.]
But I was concentrating on...' Realisation sudden[ly]
dawned. 'You saw it happening again! First Erin, th[en]
Hilary, then me... What did that nurse call you? Y[ou]
thought you were the Angel of Death?'

He smiled. 'You're alive, Delyth. No, quite the oppos[ite]
happened. In that split second I realised that all the go[od]
things in life have to be grabbed. I'd be an utter fool to l[et]
something as miraculous as you escape me. Tell me, seven[th]
daughter of seventh daughter, what do you foresee for us[?]'

'I don't need any paranormal powers to tell me that. It[']
a choice that only you can make. Perhaps I'm taking thin[gs]
for granted, but I think we could have a happy life togethe[r.]
You've had more than your share of misery—now y[ou]
could share in happiness. You've got a ready-made famil[y.]
They'll love you and I know you'll love them.'

'You're going too fast,' he told her. 'Wait a minute.' B[ut]
then he realised he didn't want to wait a minute. He too[k]
one, two, three deep breaths. 'Delyth,' he said, 'will y[ou]
marry me?'

She didn't need to think about her answer. 'Of course [I]
will,' she said. 'I couldn't imagine loving anyone mor[e,]
couldn't think of anyone who would make me more happ[y.]
Come here and kiss me.'

She slid down the bed, her long hair coiled on the pillo[w.]
'I've got a thought for you, James. I'm the seventh daught[er]

of a seventh daughter. Supposed to have powers. What if we have seven daughters?'

'So long as they are all like you,' he said, kissing her again.

MILLS & BOON®

Makes
any time
special

Enjoy a romantic novel from
Mills & Boon®

Presents...™   Enchanted™   Temptation®

Historical Romance™   Medical Romance™

MILLS & BOON®

ᴧᴧ **MEDICAL ROMANCE™**

PRACTICALLY PERFECT by Caroline Anderson

Surgeon Connie Wright found locum G.P. Patrick Durrant
deeply attractive and his small son Edward soon found a
place in her heart. But Patrick would be moving on and
Connie would be returning to London...

TAKE TWO BABIES... by Josie Metcalfe

Maddie's ex-husband had kidnapped her daughter and she
was distraught. When Dr William Ward was so supportive,
Maddie knew this man was for her...

TENDER LIAISON by Joanna Neil

Dr Daniel Maitland doesn't believe Dr Emma Barnes will stay in
his practice—nor does he believe Emma when she says he has a
lot of love to give!

A HUGS-AND-KISSES FAMILY by Meredith Webber
Bundles of Joy

Dr Angus McLeod had never stopped loving Jen, his only
thought to woo and win her all over again. Discovering Jen
was pregnant was *such* a shock!

Available from 1st October 1999

MILLS & BOON®

Next Month's Romance Titles

♡

Each month you can choose from a wide variety of romance novels from Mills & Boon®. Below are the new titles to look out for next month from the Presents...™ and Enchanted™ series.

Presents...™

A RELUCTANT MISTRESS	Robyn Donald
THE MARRIAGE RESOLUTION	Penny Jordan
THE FINAL SEDUCTION	Sharon Kendrick
THE REVENGE AFFAIR	Susan Napier
THE HIRED HUSBAND	Kate Walker
THE MILLIONAIRE AFFAIR	Sophie Weston
THE BABY VERDICT	Cathy Williams
THE IMPATIENT GROOM	Sara Wood

Enchanted™

THE DADDY DILEMMA	Kate Denton
AND MOTHER MAKES THREE	Liz Fielding
TO CLAIM A WIFE	Susan Fox
THE BABY WISH	Myrna Mackenzie
MARRYING A MILLIONAIRE	Laura Martin
THE HUSBAND CAMPAIGN	Barbara McMahon
TEMPTING A TYCOON	Leigh Michaels
MAIL-ORDER MARRIAGE	Margaret Way

On sale from 1st October 1999

H1 9909

Available at most branches of WH Smith, Tesco, Asda, Martins, Borders, Easons, Volume One/James Thin and most good paperback bookshops